Stories
for the
Thoughtful Young

Sit with me, come and see,
It is time for a story.
Take my hand, come and look,
It is time for a book.
Sit with me, come and see,
Snuggle close together.
Take my hand, come and look.
Let us share this good book!

Storytime Song
by Sheila Kerwin
Sung to the tune of Brahms' "Lullaby"

Also from B Cubed Press

Alternative Truths

More Alternative Truths: Tales From the Resistance

After the Orange: Ruin and Recovery

Alternative Theology

EndGames

Digging Up My Bones,

by Gwyndyn T. Alexander

Firedancer,

by S.A. Bolich

Alternative Apocalypse

OZ is Burning

Stories
for the
Thoughtful Young

Edited by
Diana Payton and Bob Brown

Cover Design
Bob Brown

Published by

B Cubed Press
Kiona, WA

Copyright

Thoughtful Young

Publisher's Introduction

As a child, I read.

I read everything I could find.

Living in a world where the television got two channels, barely, and the only screens in the house were on doors and windows, I loved the heavy dark books I found in a box in the basement.

My favorite was a thick green volume called *Prose and Poetry.* I read it through more times than I have memory of.

It was a book of stories and poems meant for another generation but I loved the words, the glossy pages, the detailed images.

Like all young readers I found reading to be a transport in time and space. A chance to stand beside Horatio on the Bridge and stride forth from Troy with Hector.

Time dims the memories of the detail, but not the pleasure of those worlds.

In this volume Diana Payton and I have the opportunity to give memories to a new generation. Stories of love and triumph and sometimes just finding the good in doing the right thing.

Experience what Diana and I already have: the joy of reading these beautiful stories for the first time and then sharing them with others, whether with your grandchild under a quilt, or gift to someone you know will find the time to visit these other worlds that these wonderful writers have conjured for us all.

Thoughtful Young

Table of Contents

Thoughtful Young

Thoughtful Young

Ballerina Scientist

Karen Thrower

Elena loved to dance and sing. She also loved all science things! Pink shoes and tutus, the process of making glue. Dancing to music with buns and measuring fluid for fun, it all brought joy to her.

At age eight when the gap in her teeth was prominent, she declared with confidence, "I know what I shall be when I grow up, I shall be a Ballerina Scientist!"

Her mom beamed with pride, with tears in her eyes. "I shall be your guide!" For she believed her clever daughter could do whatever she endeavored.

Elena danced almost every day, there was no time for horseplay. At least horseplay in ballet. After dance she'd read about the ocean and properties of motion, biology and the bones of archeology. All to feed her need to succeed, for science was reliant on her big brain becoming a super-giant!

Her arabesque went from wobbly to stationary, a glorious sight! Her understanding of chemistry from dreadful to specialty. Now nothing was beyond her grasp!

She'd plie while reciting the periodic table and fill beakers while squeaking in her sneakers. She'd twirl and make sure her goggles wouldn't jostle. Everyone noticed her fun.

She read books on Copeland and Cori, Curie and Kirkland. They were her keys to appease the unease that would creep into her sleep. Her dreams would make her dance a flop, and her chemical reactions never took off! Tumbling on stage and bungling the definition of macrophage, makes her want to disengage!

She'd wake in a panic, half manic with fear. Could she do this, her mind began to fear it was too much, being both ballerina and scientist. Should she just do one? Or none? If she didn't have science or dance, did she even stand a chance?

Her mother saw how worried she had become and, in a flurry, hurried to ease her mind. "Dear daughter, the path you are on is curved. There are many different ways to blaze your trail, though none are easy, please don't get queasy. Dance hard my little bard, and your heart will jumpstart. Learn chemistry zestfully, and your brain won't complain. And one day you will be my little Ballerina Scientist."

Her mother's words eased her panic. She wiped her tears and swallowed her fears. She would be the first ballerina scientist! She would prove that with the right groove, science and dance were both things she could do.

When Elena was grown and lived in an old brownstone, her love of ballet had led her to Broadway. Singing and dancing, twirling and song had become part of her life with hardly any strife. On the wall above her couch, a degree in Chemistry would vouch, she had indeed become the world's first Ballerina Scientist. Swirling chemicals by day and dancing by night, her life was indeed very bright. For she never forgot the words of her mother: "Dance hard my little bard and your heart will jumpstart. Learn chemistry, zestfully and your brain won't complain. And one day you will be my little Ballerina Scientist."

The Goblin Knight

Aimee Ogden

There had never been a goblin knight before. That was why Qimzik had to be the first.

He was supposed to be working down in the cornfield. His brothers and sisters were there, walking between the towering rows of field corn and crushing the tips of cobs to kill the bore-worms. No one noticed Qimzik was gone until it was too late. Only his youngest sister knew his plans. She agreed to cover for him, as he would need to walk three towns over to earn his place at the Academy.

Qimzik still wore his canvas fieldwork gloves and despite skipping the day's labor, he was hot and tired. On his head, he wore the painted goblin helmet and war mask that had belonged to his grandfather, not a knight, but a warrior feared by bandits and robbers alike. Qimzik wanted to be the first goblin knight, but it would be best if no one knew about the "goblin" part until after he'd won his admission.

By the time he trudged into the town of Greenwick, the sun was drawing close to the top of the sky. A tangled cluster of young people collected in the open grassy fields just east of town. Along one side stretched a rope. Behind it, families chattered and waved at the candidates assembling on the field. Qimzik's stomach twisted. Did anyone know he was gone yet?

It didn't matter. He checked his helmet's fit once more and walked onto the field to register his entry.

A table stood at one end of the field; not really a table, more like a few old planks balanced between a pair of sawhorses. The knight sitting there didn't even look up at Qimzik. She had gray streaks in her hair, and ink smudges all over her fingers. "Name? Age?"

"Uh ..." Qimzik swallowed. "Tim. Tim ... Tick. Eleven years old."

The knight scribbled furiously on the paper in front of her. "Join the queue on the right, please. You'll be evaluated by Sir Teppin."

"Thank you." Qimzik shuffled into his place in line. Sir Qimzik. He liked the sound of that. Sir Tick, not as much.

"Nice helmet," said the boy ahead of Qimzik in line; his dark eyes barely peeped out from under his thick black hair. His clothes were newer than Qimzik's, and his belt buckle looked like real brass. "Did you get that from a dead goblin?"

Technically, he had. "Yes," he hedged.

The boy nodded with satisfaction. "My granddad has one of those at home from the Frontier Wars. He killed hundreds of goblins! Not that that's hard." The boy stuck out his hand. Qimzik wanted to slap it away, but instead he shook it. "My name's Marit."

"I'm ... Tim." Marit seemed to be expecting something more, and Qimzik's mouth dried out as he realized what that probably was. "Yes, um, there's a goblin family in my town too. My friends and I like to ride our horses over their fields and trample their corn, because they're too scared to stop us." Marit laughed, and under his mask, Qimzik's teeth bared in something more like a grimace than a smile.

"That sounds horrible." Marit and Qimzik turned. Behind Qimzik, a girl had arrived. She had dark brown skin and tightly curled black hair combed back away from her face and pulled into a tight braid she wore all along the top of her head like a crown. Her clothes were worn and flecked with what might have been flour, but her boots were new: someone's gift for the day, maybe. Qimzik swallowed back both a quick retort and a surge of jealousy. "Knights don't pick on the helpless. Not true knights," said the girl.

"True knights don't get squeamish about a fight." Merit spat on the ground, making the girl step back in her shiny new boots. "Who are you, anyway? The baker's girl? Do you even know which end of the sword to hold?"

"I'm Ria," she said. "And I don't care who you are, because you're awful."

Before Merit could open his mouth to argue, a booming voice rolled out. "Belin Nishol! Marit Ertran! Tim Tick!"

There were more names bellowed out, but the ground seemed to yawn out from beneath Qimzik's feet once he heard his own made-up name called. This was real now.

"You're up next for the strength trials. This way!"

When Qimzik's legs felt like they worked again, he trotted after the other applicants. They followed a man in full leather armor embossed all over with gold and red dragons. This must be Sir Teppin. The knight was tall and narrow-shouldered, but his voice was deep enough to carry across the field as he called the applicants' names. As he finished, he looked up from his list, and paused when he saw Qimzik's helmet. "That's, er ..."

"It's good luck," Qimzik squeaked, and Sir Teppin's booming laugh made his knees knock together.

"Keep it, then! But you'll need more than luck today, lad."

Sir Teppin explained what would happen during the physical trials. The applicants had to run around the field twice, then hop over a series of hurdles. Finally, they would scale a wooden wall and climb back down the other side with the use of several heavy ropes.

Qimzik ran as fast he could, which wasn't very fast. Goblins were top-heavy creatures, with stumpy legs and thick upper bodies, not well suited for speed. But his physique turned to his advantage when he reached the hurdles, where he could use the strength in his shoulders to lever himself over each barrier. Other, faster runners tried and failed to leap over on the power of their legs alone.

He sailed easily up the wall, just behind Merit— whose boot he saw stamp down on Ria's fingers just as she reached the top. Ria yelped as Merit disappeared over the wall, but Qimzik grabbed her wrist before she could fall.

"Thanks," she said breathlessly, as he pulled her up so she could straddle the top of the wall. Then she too disappeared. Qimzik scrambled to follow her.

Qimzik came in toward the top third of the physical trials; not bad, he thought. But up next were horsemanship trials. Qimzik's family had never had the money for a horse! He found himself with his rear end in the dirt shortly after first settling it in the saddle. He only barely managed to keep his helmet from flying off.

He snagged his horse's reins as they went by and heaved himself back into the saddle as the great smelly beast skittered underneath him.

"Psst!" Qimzik glanced around. Ria was astride a speckled mare, taking a leisurely stroll up and down the length of the field. "Just relax. Pretend you're a sack of flour. Just let yourself sag into the saddle."

Qimzik tried to relax, but the horse had other ideas in mind. He kept his seat for a little longer this time, but still wound up grounded again before long. When he managed to regain his feet, Sir Teppin was collecting his horse's reins. "I can try again!" he said, and wasn't sure whether he wanted to hear the knight say yes or no more.

Teppin gave him a half-smile as he led the horse away. "Not necessary, Tim. Almost time for the last trial, so wait on the sideline for my orders."

Qimzik obeyed, but the next time he looked back at Sir Teppin, the man was scrawling busily on his paper. Qimzik didn't like to guess what kind of notes he was making.

Before long, the other boys and girls were all waiting for instructions alongside Qimzik. He wondered what to expect. But finally, Sir Teppin put aside his notes and peered down at the gathered group. "The last trial," he said, "has always been the one that cuts closest to what it means to truly be a knight. For this trial, we ask you to do the simplest and most difficult thing of all: something brave."

Something brave? What could he do? Qimzik racked his brain. Balance a sword on his nose? Climb to the top of the physical-trial wall and do jumping jacks?

"Where's the nearest goblin?" Merit said loudly, interrupting Qimzik's thoughts. "And the nearest sword?" There was a round of giggles.

Ria rounded on him. "Brave doesn't always have to mean fighting. Brave means doing something you're scared of. It's not brave to hurt someone you know you can hurt." Sir Teppin stepped between Ria and Merit, and gave them both a low rebuke that Qimzik couldn't make out.

Somehow, Ria's words stung almost as much as Merit's. But before he could open his mouth, Sir Teppin's voice rang out again. "Tim Tick, you'll go first. How will you prove your bravery?"

Qimzik shuffled forward. His palms were sweaty, but he knew what he had to do. He let his gloves fall to the grass, then reached up and pulled the helmet off his head, revealing his bumpy gray skin and pointed ears. There was a gasp, and the circle of space around him opened up even farther. He felt his cheeks blush a muddy brown, but he kept his eyes on the ground. "I guess I'm the nearest goblin. I'm not here to fight anyone, though. I just wanted to be a knight. To protect my family, and other people's families." He couldn't help himself adding, "Even Merit's."

Qimzik felt a shove on his shoulder, and he stumbled and fell, knees bruising against the hard soil. When he looked up from the ground, one of Sir Teppin's thin hands was wrapped around Merit's arm. He didn't look happy, and neither did Merit. "That's quite enough from you, boy. Come back next year to try again, if you've grown up a bit before then." Teppin gave him a little push that sent him hurrying off to the sideline rope, where a disappointed family waited.

A hand appeared in front of Qimzik's face. Ria smiled, a little nervously, when he put his hand in hers, and pulled him to his feet. "I've never met a goblin before, up close," she said. "I should have guessed. Sorry."

Qimzik looked at the ring of shocked faces and grimaces all around them. "Don't be sorry," he said, and dusted himself off. "I should probably go."

"Yes, you should," said Sir Teppin. "You'll need to—"

Ria drew herself up as tall as she could. "Tim was as brave as you could ask! He only came in so far back in the first trial because he stopped to help me, and, well, anyone can learn to ride a horse!" She folded her arms. "If I win a place, I want him to have it instead. I'll try again next year."

Sir Teppin coughed. "As I was saying, Tim— is that your real name?"

"Qimzik," Qimzik told his boots.

"Qimzik, then. You should be getting along to speak to the quartermaster to make arrangements for travel." He ripped one of his sheets of paper in half, scribbled a flourish at the bottom, and handed it to Qimzik. "Your parents will have to sign it, of course. Oh, and here." He repeated the same action with another sheet of paper, and passed this one to Ria, whose face was as dark as boiled beets. "You ought to do the same." His face crooked in the briefest of smiles, then crashed back to solemnity. "Right! Rynale Rodap, you're up!"

Qimzik followed Ria in a daze, his feet all but floating above the ground. Ria was babbling happily at him, dragging him along to the quartermaster's table, but a sudden realization dropped him like an anchor. "I can't," he said suddenly, and let go of her hand. "I can't. My parents will have to sign it, and they're..."

"Coming to talk to you," Ria finished, and pointed. "Or at least, I guess that's them? There aren't any other goblins here that I can see."

Qimzik spun, just in time for his youngest sister to fling her arms around him and whisper in his ear: "I'm no good at keeping secrets." Then he was wrapped up in the arms of a laughing, crying goblin horde.

The Wizard and the Woke

James Blakey

Chris Duffy was the best baseball player in town. So it was no surprise that when Angel Hernandez hung a fat curve over the plate, Chris walloped it. The ball arced over the left field fence, flew across Barack Obama Street, and crashed through the window of a house.

The Wizard's house.

"Oh, man," said Jerry Stein. "You did it this time, Chris! Better run before the Wizard gets you."

Chris completed the circuit around the bases and shook their head. "Nope. My parents taught me to be responsible for my actions. I'm going over to apologize."

"You can't go alone." Darius Jackson frowned. "That old Wizard is crazy. Pulled a gun on me and my brother last year when we knocked on his door for trick-or-treat."

"We should all go," said Jennifer Chen. "Friends stick together."

Players from both teams nodded agreement, dropped their gloves, and walked with Chris to the Wizard's house.

By the time the teenagers arrived, the Wizard was outside, inspecting the shattered glass. His thin, white hair stuck out from beneath his red ball cap. A Ted Nugent t-shirt strained to cover his massive belly. He held a beer can one hand and a cigarette in the other. In the driveway sat a mud-splattered F-250 covered with bumper stickers, most supportive of the Second Amendment.

"Which one of you troublemakers broke my window?" The Wizard jabbed his cigarette at Hernandez. "I bet it was the illegal."

"No person is illegal," said Angel.

"I did it." Chris stepped forward. "I apologize."

The Wizard looked from the ball field to his house and squinted at Chris. "A girl hit a ball that far?"

"I'm non-binary. My pronouns are they/their/them."

"Pronouns? What nonsense is this?" sputtered the Wizard. "And apologies won't fix my window."

"I know." Chris took a deep breath. "I'll pay for it."

"You mean your daddy will pay for it," sneered the Wizard.

Chris shook their head. "I don't have a dad. I have two moms."

The Wizard rolled his eyes. "Of course you do. But you won't learn responsibility by having your mommies pay."

"It will be my money. I work weekends at the organic farmer's market. I was saving up to donate to Planned Parenthood. Responsibility is important."

The Wizard slurped his beer. "You need to do more than take responsibility. There needs to be a deterrent so you'll think twice before you destroy more property. You're a fit young girl, w—"

"Person," interrupted Chris. "I'm a person. Please, don't misgender me."

"Whatever. I know just the spell to teach you a lesson. It'll be a shame when you gain all that weight and lose your figure. The Wizard smiled, displaying crooked teeth, and began the incantation.

"We don't fatshame!" yelled Joseph Running Wolf.

"Fine." The Wizard glared at Chris. "Then, we'll something about your clear skin and high cheekbones. A curse of disfigurement is ex—"

"That's lookism!" shouted Marta Veranakova.

"I don't believe this," muttered the Wizard.

"#BelieveAllWomen," said Preneeth Denduluri.

The Wizard took a drag on his cigarette. "Suppose your legs no longer functioned? You'd spend the rest of your life confined to a wheelchair."

Chris crossed their arms. "We celebrate all different forms of ability."

The Wizard sighed. "Okay, a prolonged illness. No lasting effects, but the treatments will cost tens, if not hundreds, of thousands of dollars. Your family, <u>your mothers</u>, will be bankrupt, destitute. Then you'll respect other people's property."

"We have single-payer healthcare now," said Muhammad Omer.

"Single-payer?" The Wizard turned pale. "What the hell happened to this country?"

Chris' eyes darted to the faded "Hands Off <u>MY</u> Medicare" bumper sticker on the pick-up. "Can't I just pay for the broken window and call it even?"

The Wizard guzzled the rest of his beer and tossed the can. It bounced off the vertical exhaust stack and clattered in the truck bed.. "Bah, I've had enough of this." He turned to go inside.

"But don't you want your money?" asked Chris.

"No!" the Wizard roared. "What I want is for you kids to get off my lawn!"

Thoughtful Young

Beyond the Wall

Shelby Workman

The girl goes to the wall.

It is winter. She wears her red cloak because it is the finest piece of clothing she has, and it is all she has to keep her warm. She's going to her father's grave.

It's not a proper grave. Many died of the cold and the wolves while building the wall. She remembers the day her mother opened the door to a solemn-faced man and collapsed on the floor before he spoke a word. The wall is her father's tomb, his skeleton buried inside it, along with so many others. *It's an honor to have died in service to the village*, the village's Master always says when he stands on his podium. *It is an honor. Their families are very proud, and those who died know what an honor it was. At night their ghosts hover over my bed and whisper into my ears how proud they are, how grateful they are to have made such a powerful sacrifice for the good of the village. We do what we must to keep the wolves out.*

There have always been wolves. Wolves circling the houses, sniffing for a way inside. Wolves nosing open doors in the night and gobbling up babies in cribs, raiding pantries, dragging screaming men into the woods.

The wall keeps them out, the people say, the Master says.

Her mother, who's the closest the village has to a true witch, made a protective charm for her: a tiny wolf's head fashioned from silver, with emerald eyes. Whenever the tax collectors came, she hid it away. She woke this morning to find it gone, snatched from her throat while she slept. What else could have crept in, soundless as smoke, but a wolf?

She is without her charm, but she has her mother's hunting rifle. There's no food but there are many guns in the village. So many. People sit beside their cold hearths, empty bellies rumbling like avalanches, guns on their laps while they listen for scratching at the door, for the panting of blood-reeking breath.

The Master says, *These wolves, they're in our beds, disguised as our grandmothers. You see their teeth. They eat our girls. There's nothing they won't eat.*

Before the wall, the village's men and some women went into the woods to hunt the wolves. They burned miles of forests. The girl was young then, but she remembers the skies boiled black with smoke, the fire a spiky crown above the trees, red as sunset, and the taste of ash scorching her throat. The hunters came back with piles of ragged pelts and with fingers and limbs missing, their faces gaunt, their feet wrapped in bloody rags. *It was the wolves,* says the Master. *These brave people fought the wolves and these are the noble scars they show for it. Our battle against these dangerous beasts never ends.* Whenever he says this, there's always a hunter or two beside him, coat sleeves dangling empty, leaning on wooden crutches. They say nothing while the Master talks. *These brave men and women,* the Master says, *are heroes and we honor them.*

They are our heroes and we honor them, parrot the villagers. But the girl always sees these hunters huddling alone in unswept corners and in doorways, rubbing the stumps of their missing fingers and staring hauntedly at nothing.

"Don't listen," a rag-footed man once whispered to her before her mother could whisk her away. "It was frostbite that took my toes, not wolves. Our friends fell down dead, and we ate them where they lay. The only wolves we killed tried to run away." She never saw that man again; the corner where he sat was empty the next day. *The wolves must have gotten him,* people say, the Master says.

The wall keeps the wolves out, but they still find ways inside.

The cold sinks its fangs into her bones. The wind gusts through the rags of her clothes; even her treasured cloak is tattered, torn from snagging on brambles when she goes to gather the roots and herbs for her mother's potions. It's the coldest winter anyone can remember and there's no wood for fireplaces. The only wood is in the forest, outside the wall. Crops wither in the frost.

Must be careful, must be quick. It's nearly curfew. Her red cloak will give her away. She slips past the graveyard that is wider than the village, the mounds piled with stones to keep beasts from digging at them. Past the small houses with the cracked walls and decaying roofs. What little anyone has goes to the wall. It must stay up, must be kept from crumbling down. Everyone dreads the tax collector's knock more than the howling in the night. Even the men who patrol the village streets, the new rifles in their hands oiled to a shine, have thin faces and hunger-dulled eyes. *We must have the wall,* the Master says. *We must have weapons.*

The wall looms ahead. It flutters with memorial ribbons and the husks of long-dead flowers, names scratched into the stones. She could tip her head up until she falls backward and still not see the top.

The Master once vowed he would build a memorial, a proper one, for those who perished while building the wall. Taxes went up, and everyone in the village scraped together what they could for the Master's men at the door. No memorial was ever built, but the Master wears fine furs, his fingers glittering with rings.

The wall is massive but it's cracked, the stones fitted crudely together. The wind howls through it like a starving pack. The girl finds this odd. The village feeds the wall before all things, yet it grows as ragged as the people. Only the Master grows fat.

Good girls shouldn't think on such things, Mother says.

Things are good here, people whisper as they hack at the frozen ground to bury the dead. *The wall keeps us safe. The Master keeps us safe.*

But some in the village mutter there used to be paths in the woods that lead a to cities and towns bursting with riches, ripe for trading. They mutter that the wall cuts off the fields, and so the goats and cows grow gaunt in the barren pastures and give no milk. It takes days to walk anywhere; those who try, return with hands black with frostbite and having been forced to eat their own wares.

The Master says that the cities don't have walls and so are overrun with wolves. *They have nothing left. Nothing to trade with us, nothing they can possibly share with us. They don't have walls. The wolves take everything they have. They have absolutely nothing.*

When the Master talks, his sentences go around and around like this, like vultures circling. Sometimes he will stop in the midst of a speech and stare up at the air as if the words he has forgotten are floating above his head, waiting for him to snatch them back. *He is getting old,* people whisper, fearful. *Who will protect us from the wolves when he's gone? Who will keep the wall standing?*

It's nearly dark. The girl maps the stones with her hands until she finds the familiar grooves of her father's name. She has not come to visit. She has come to say farewell.

When she woke to find the charm missing, she should have run screaming an alarm through the streets. Alerted the Master. Rallied the hunters into the woods to slaughter the wolves and bring back everything that was stolen.

But is she not the best shot of her age in the village? Is she not the brave one, the one who ventures out after nightfall to gather herbs for her mother, risking her neck to wolves and curfew-enforcers alike?

The wolves took her charm. They have taken everything. They will not have this.

There's a crack in the wall. She finds it easily. Just big enough for a wolf to slip through. Or a child.

It's a tight squeeze, but she is thin.

The forest is vast and fire scarred. Jagged stumps bristling from the snow like broken teeth. The winter-stripped trees bare and black as though the flames swept through just yesterday. Branches claw at her. She grips her gun tightly and scans the snow for prints or scat. She watches the shadows for red eyes.

There are paths, buried in frost and ashen carpets of dead leaves. She closes her eyes and chooses one, following some inner compass like a thread wound through a labyrinth. She'll find the thief with her necklace gleaming at its mangy throat, shoot it and take its skin home for a trophy. Or perhaps for a cloak, to replace the threadbare red.

She walks and walks. She licks snow for water and digs with her fingers for roots, their skins bitter with dirt. Once she catches a hare and strips the pelt and devours it raw, afraid the smell of cooking meat might lure predators. The cold numbs her hands until she can barely feel the gun held in them. When she stops to rest, she huddles beneath her ragged cape, clutching her rifle like a doll.

No living wolves prowl near, but there are plenty of ghosts. Darting around the trees like tails of mist, the bare trunks visible right through them. The girl doesn't waste her bullets, knowing they will only pass through the ghosts like air, but their jaws may still rend her flesh.

"Even the dead have teeth," Mother once said, while she fastened the charm at her daughter's throat.

But they do not bite. They follow alongside, brushing against her, cold as clouds. The wind moans, echoing the memory of their moon-lifted voices, their agony. She keeps her eyes fixed ahead and thinks, *I am brave. I am brave.*

Just when she can't walk any farther, she reaches a clearing in the woods.

There's a hut. Small but well-kept, its roof whole and unpatched. The ghosts of the wolves block her way, hackles bristling, their growls sawing into her.

Her charm is inside. She feels it calling to her. If she takes another step, she'll be torn apart.

She raises her gun, even though it does her no good. "Let me pass."

"We cannot," says the biggest of the ghosts.

The girl nearly drops the rifle. All the stories she has heard never spoke of wolves that talk, alive or dead.

"If I step closer," she asks, "will you eat me?"

"I never ate a human while I lived," it says, "and I can hardly start now."

"Nor I, nor I," the others chorus.

"That's a lie." If she keeps them talking, perhaps she can trick them into letting her sneak by. "You come into our village and feast on us all the time. We had to build a wall to keep you out."

"Does your wall keep us out, or does it keep you in? Don't lie, you've never stepped outside your home before, have you?"

Another says, "When we lived, we knew to avoid places where men kept guns beside their beds. *You* hunted *us*."

"You ate our livestock." That, she knows, is true.

"You stripped the woods of our prey, what did you expect?"

"You slaughtered us with bullets and with fire. You burned our home."

She says, "You stole my charm."

"Ask that magpie Master of yours where it is," says the biggest ghost, lips curled in contempt.

"Ask *yourself*," a third pipes up, "if we are the cause of all your misery, and we are dead, why does your misery persist? Why do you starve within the safety of your wall? That Master of yours never goes hungry, does he? You call us your destruction, but you hardly need our help."

She gnaws her lip. "What do you know of us?"

"Your Master comes here often. This place is his. It was he who bound us to it."

That gets her attention. "What binds you?"

"A curse. Our bones are inside. As long as they are here, we cannot leave."

She lowers her rifle. "A bargain, then?"

The big one snorts. "What can you do for us?"

"I can free you. If there is a curse, destroying the bones should end it. I'm a witch's daughter. I know how these things work."

"You're a selfish little thing. Tell the truth." Their eyes pierce her. "Why have you come?"

She doesn't flinch. "I want what's mine."

"So take it."

She steps forward. As one, the wolves step aside, clearing a path for her to the door.

Inside, she finds a hoard fit for a dragon.

Hills of gold, dazzling to the eye as sunshine. Glittering jewels. Silver. Dented copper pots.

She searches. Here is Widow Rosaleen's ring with the damson-purple stone. Young Mason's gold brooch. A sea-stone necklace meant for a new bride. She remembers seeing them pressed into the tax collectors' palms by their weeping owners.

At last, she finds a glint of emerald and silver. She snatches it.

Then she sits back on her heels, the charm in her hand. She stares at it for a long time.

The wall needs your jewels, the Master says, while his tax collectors swarm the village like locusts. *Anything you have. We must have mortar and stone to keep it standing. Sacrifices must be made.*

The Master, with his fine thick furs and seam-bursting gut. What other lies has he told?

She stares at her pendant. She should leave. Go back to the village, say nothing of this.

She *should.*

She won't.

Using her cloak as a sack, she bundles as much treasure as she can and carries it outside, back and forth like drawing well-water to fill her mother's cauldron, until the hut is empty. The sun is nearly risen by the time she finishes. She rests for a bit, then climbs the rafters and rips up the floorboards. Worming her fingers into every cranny, every crack, searching for anything she might have missed. She uncovers the pearly gleam of bone. Ribs and vertebrae inside the walls, toothy skulls grinning in the dark underneath the floor.

She burns the hut. All is cold and sodden, but she manages; her mother taught her how to light fires even in pouring rain. She sets it ablaze and watches as it crumbles and blackens, the walls peeling back like bark to bare the bones built into them. As the flames crackle, she turns to the wolves.

They sit watching her. Their fire-lit eyes like a procession of funeral candles.

"You're free." It's all she can think to say.

Like a flash flood in reverse, they vanish into the forest.

The girl follows the path home. She walks slowly, feet dragging with exhaustion. The rifle is heavy; she lets it fall from her numbed hands and leaves it behind.

At home, all is ruin, all is dust.

The wall has been knocked down. She steps over the rubble of it, imagining how the wolves must have smashed through, their spectral bodies flooding into the town as if from a burst dam. The streets are empty; the villagers peer from their windows with rabbit-round eyes.

She walks until she reaches what remains of the Master's mansion. A grand house of glass-smooth stone and rich bloodred wood, it had towered over its sad hovel neighbors. Only splinters are left.

Of the Master, there is no trace.

An echo lingers in the air over the debris –a wolf's howl, or a man's final shriek.

All around her there are footsteps, fearful whispers. *"What has happened?" "How did this happen?"*

The girl wonders what will become of them now. She'll lead them to the gold, tell them the truth of the Master and the wolves. She wonders if they will listen to her, or if another Master will stand above the village and preach lies of fear and hate before the sun sets. She doesn't know.

But there are paths, and she knows which she will take.

The Last Child

Paula Hammond

Cuddle close, My Love. The shutters are locked. The candles are lit. The world outside is nothing now, except what we choose to make of it.

So let me tell you a tale. A tale from times long gone, when the gods walked amongst us, and a dragon slept beneath every mountain.

Once upon a time—because that's how all really old tales begin—Llŷr, god of the sea, made the barren lands flower. Nurturing and feeding us all with his transformative touch.

Humans were his children first. If not in blood, in care: thriving on what his oceans brought us.

Later, Llŷr had children of his own. Ellyllon and gwyllion. Spirits and sidhe. Protectors of home, hearth, and harvest. Sprites who guarded the holy wells, springs, and lakes.

Like their father, each little god and goddess had names which revealed the gifts they brought to the land and its people. And we remembered each of them: at dawn, at dusk, and at the turning of the seasons.

Later still, Llŷr had one last child. A singular child, unlike those who had gone before. A child who offered her people more than fire, and water, and food for the belly. That child had no name that mortal tongues may speak, but was known by many. Wonder. Imagination. Magic.

Now, Llŷr loved his children equally, as a good father should. Yet this last child seemed especially blessed. True, she had her father's stormy ways. Like all children, she could be wild, impulsive; throwing her power around in gleeful gusts that rippled reality and made people doubt their senses.

She had her dark times too, when she glowered and tested her father's patience. Times when she called the wyvern out to ride, when she conjured the death-bringer—

21

Angelystor—from beneath the sacred yew, when she made the skeleton trees dance. Those were the days when we clung to our charms of snake-stone and mistletoe, placed protective lanterns in our windows, and wished for less capricious gods.

Later, as she grew into her powers, this last child gave us wondrous things. Oh, My Love, as we sit here watching the smoke from the candle craft its wispy, little clouds, I hope you can see how it once was—when the magic was everywhere. In the flickering fire, in the entrails of animals, in the casting of bones. In the mist, and in the moonlight, and in the new-born day.

When we looked into the chill lakes of our homeland valleys, it wasn't ourselves we saw, but our Otherworld twins, staring out from the realm of enchantment, daring us to believe. And we did believe. We believed so hard in the magic, that we could almost reach out and touch it.

In this land, a simple song could wake the dead or lull the living to sleep.

In this land, fairy dancers left golden rings etched in dewy grass.

In this land, Jack-in-the-Green strode through the twilight, with hounds baying at his heels.

In this land, men were heroes, horses were steeds, birds were messengers of hope and harbingers of doom.

The last child of Llŷr made our barren minds flower, nurturing, feeding, transforming all with her thaumaturgic touch.

We were her children, then, as much as her father's. If not in blood, in spirit: thriving on what she taught us.

Once, we were such frail things. Unsure of ourselves and our place in the world. But this last child taught us how to see things anew. How to peer into the dark shadows. How to revel in nature's wonders. She showed us that dreams mattered. That they could change who we were. They could change the world itself. It was then we learnt that we had power of our own.

So we took these gifts and crafted worlds of our own. But we were not gods. We could not re-shape the stuff of creation, so we made our realities with ink and parchment, with voice and song, with pigment daubed on stone and etched on skin. And in these new worlds, the old were wise, visionaries spoke truths, bards forged kingdoms, and healers chased away the darkness.

Oh, My Love, it is true these times long gone were far from perfect. They were at times harsh and cruel. There was want and loss. Yes, and hate too. And perhaps it was the hate which made it so easy for us to forget Llŷr, god of the sea. To forget his little gods and goddesses, the ellyllon and gwyllion, the spirits, and the sidhe. To forget his last child. To forget her gifts.

But, because we had become so used to creating our own worlds, we went a step further and created our own god. Now, it is Money, god of man, who makes the barren lands flower, nurturing, feeding, transforming all with his empirical touch.

Later, Money, god of man, also had children of his own. Angels and demons. Prophets and profiteers. Despots and dictators who claimed the wells, lakes, and rivers, for themselves. Who took away our land and our song, and told us to kneel and obey.

In this land, we must learn to be realistic.

In this land, we must put away childish things.

In this land, we need to look after our own.

We are his children now, if not in blood, in fact: thriving on what his ones and zeros bring us.

He is a good god, this Money. Protector of home, hearth, and harvest. Guardian of people and planet. He fills our bellies, makes the blind see, the lame walk.

Like all the gods, he is dangerous too, this god of man. Capable of destroying as well as creating. He offers us truth, order, and certainty. He helps those who help themselves. He fills our days with so much getting and wanting that, in the end, there is little time anything else. And he does all of this without the need for belief.

But we do believe. We believe so hard, in the here-and-now, in the cold, hard cash, and the cold, hard facts, in what can be bought and sold. We seem to need nothing else.

Come, My Love, we're almost at the end of my tale. Soon it will be time to sleep. So, cuddle closer, and listen with me. What is it you hear? Is it just the storm outside, rattling at the shutters? Is it the trickle of the rain, as it hits the roof? Is it the groan of the trees as they bend in the wind? Or is it something else? Listen to it, down, in the earth. Take my hand as we fly deep, into the forgotten places. Don't be afraid. We're almost there.

See it now, that faint glow? Hear it now, that low buzz? There it is; something magical, trapped, culverted, and suffocated, buried by the centuries, but there all the same.

Time has not been kind to the last child of Llŷr, god of the sea, but part of us will always remain her children. If not in blood, in memory: craving those things that we barely recall, but which make us feel human all the same.

Once, the last child of Llŷr roared through our world like a torrent of white water. Now she's barely a stream. Barely a god at all.

Somehow, we have lost the magic and the will to believe. So she must be subtler now. Less dramatic. When she moves amongst us, it's as slights of hand, optical illusions, synchronicity. We know her in the quiet moments, in feelings of *deja vu*, that certain something just out of sight, which makes our blood race and heart pound. She seems so small, now, this last child but she's still here, never-the-less, working her charms.

In this world, a stranger's smile can lift a mood.

In this world, a helping hand can make the difference.

In this world, a selfless act can save a life.

The last child of Llŷr, god of the sea, has no name that mortal tongues can speak—but is known by many. Compassion. Empathy. Hope. And one more, still...

It is a name that you will have heard tossed away in casual moments but it's a name that still has power, if we know how to use it.

Of the many names—the many gifts—the last child shared with us; it is the most important. And you should know, oh My Darling Child, it's a name I give to you, too. That name is Love.

My Girl Cindy

Ahmed Khan

A fairy godmother's work is never done, is it?

No my dear boy, the time to propose marriage has not yet come.

I know you are nineteen, and most boys your age are already married. I also know you love Elian and she loves you. That is good. But you have yet to gain her respect, and she yours. And a relationship lasts longest when respect is mixed with love.

If you want to look at a couple that shares love and respect, just look at your grandmother and grandfather. Look how happy they are! Even now, at this age, out in the garden cavorting like two small children.

Come here dear boy, and sit by the fire beside me. I will tell you the story of the time when your grandfather first proposed to your grandmother. About fifty-five years ago it was, when your grandmother was sixteen. My, how time flies!

Looking at you always reminds me of your grandmother in her youth. You looked so much like her, well before you had this growth of hair on your face. Even your mannerisms resemble hers—the way you move your hands while you talk, the way you squat on the rug, your face shining in the firelight.

Don't be impatient. I'm coming to the story.

I know you have heard the story of your grandparents from the storytellers, but how could they know what I know?

I was with your grandmother when she was born.

I was with her when her mother died, and her father married another woman.

I was with her as she grew up into a beautiful woman. I was the one who gave her the glass slippers, and I was with her when she first refused Prince Charming's marriage proposal.

Your grandmother has become a part of many stories. I've heard and read them all.

On one end are the ones where she's nothing but a passive doormat of a victim. On the other end are the ones where she's a vengeful harpy, who, as soon as she marries Charming, has her stepmother and stepsisters put to horrendous death.

None of the versions are true. None of the versions portray your grandmother's strengths, her intelligence, her liveliness, her individuality. Did any storyteller ever tell you Cinderella once frightened her stepmother near to death by putting a mouse in the cookie jar?

Did you know that Cinderella's stepsisters weren't always bad? Mostly it was their mother. Now she was evil, pure and simple. But the girls. No. Once, when Cinderella fell ill and ran a high fever, her stepsisters sat by the side of her bed the night through, applying cold towels to her brow until the fever broke.

Did the storytellers tell you that?

Do you remember your great aunts? Cinderella helped them marry well, and they lived quite happy lives, particularly after their mother died.

There you go, being impatient again. This is one trait in which you resemble your grandfather and not your grandmother.

The story I want to tell you begins at the point when Cindy passed the test of the glass slipper, and that charming prince called Prince Charming proposed marriage to her.

What did she do?

She told that boy, "I will marry you, but you have to pass a test, too."

The entourage of Prince Charming was shocked. A common girl like Cinderella wanting to test their prince! What audacity!

But Cindy was not a common girl. The prince knew this, and was proud of the fact, and agreed to be tested.

You look surprised.

You don't know much about your grandfather, do you? Again, it's the fault of those storytellers. They make him appear so one-dimensional.

Now then, where was I? Ah, yes. So then Cindy went to an old trunk, opened it, and pulled out an old, tattered pair of boots. She carried the boots to the Prince and said: "I'll marry you if these boots fit you."

The courtiers gasped in utter shock and dismay. Prince Charming took one look at the old boots and smiled.

And now, I'm sure you want to know the story behind the old pair of boots. Of course I know that story. Didn't I tell you I know a lot about Cinderella's life?

The story is quite simply told.

As you know, Cinderella's stepmother used to send her out on all sorts of tiring errands. These errands often took her through a farm, and in the course of these errands, she became friends with the family that lived on the farm.

The family consisted of just three members: the farmer, his wife, and their son, who was about two years old. They were a kind and hearty family, and Cindy always liked to stop at the farm and chat with the farmer's wife. She grew quite fond of the little boy, too.

One day, she and the farmer's wife were sitting on the grass by the fence and chatting. The little boy was playing close by. Absorbed in their conversation, they didn't notice the boy slip past the fence and wander out on the road by the farm.

It happened, just at that moment, a carriage came down that road, drawn by four horses in full gallop. The driver of the carriage gave a shout even as he pulled on his reins. Cindy and the farmer's wife raised their heads and looked and screamed. The little boy was directly in the path of the carriage, and the carriage was coming on so fast there was no way for the driver to stop it before it hit the boy.

The boy's mother fainted with fright. So, Cindy was the only one who saw what happened next. Almost like a miracle, a young man, dressed like a shepherd, leaped out of the bushes at the side of the road, swept the little boy in his arms, and rolled to safety on the other side of the road. The driver of the carriage, seeing that the boy was safe, went on without stopping.

Cinderella ran to the roadside. The boy was standing there, crying with shock, and there was no sign of the young shepherd who had saved him, except for a pair of old boots that had dropped off his feet during the rescue operation. Without a reason she could explain to me later, Cindy brought the old boots home and hid them in her trunk.

It was these boots that she had brought out to test the prince.

Good for Charming, the boots fit nicely.

And so they have been living happily ever after.

Take my advice—propose marriage to Elian only when the boots fit.

Madame Sophie and the Ghost

Sara L. Uckelman

Three things defined Madame Sophie: she was French, she was a woman, and she was a scientist. Now the first might be counted as a point in her favor, but the other two certainly were strikes against her. For, as any man in France at that time could tell you, there was no such thing as a woman scientist. Women couldn't be scientists. It was unnatural. Unbecoming. Inappropriate. Wholly unthinkable. Ask anyone in the Académie des Sciences, they could tell you–for look around the Académie, and you will not find a single woman!

But Madame Sophie was too stubborn to be told what to do by a man, and she studied and read and learned and watched and did everything a scientist did–except, of course, what she did was not science, couldn't be science, because science was something that only men could do.

Madame Sophie may have studied and learned and read many things, but her particular interest was in the science of communication, and through many years of hard work, she taught herself how to speak to anyone and anything–to people, to animals, even to ghosts.

In truth, it was not hard to learn to speak to ghosts, if one were patient and willing to sit and listen. Madame Sophie was not surprised that few men had mastered the art, for few men were patient or willing to sit and listen, at least not to others. They were far too interested in listening to themselves.

But Madame Sophie would wait, and listen, and listen again, and so she learned all the words that the ghosts would say to no one else, particularly the words no woman ghost would ever say to a man.

One day Madame Sophie met a ghost with a particularly interesting story to tell, for the sad soul's story was much like Madame Sophie's own. The ghost, when she had been alive, had lived in far-away Greece, long, long ago, and she too had been a scientist. She'd studied mathematics with Archimedes, logic with Chrysippus, geography and astronomy with Eratosthenes. But though she had studied with these greatest of ancient scientists, no one was willing to credit any of her discoveries, and no pupil came to study with her–not when they could study with a man instead. It was as if her voice could be heard by no one–no one, but Sophie.

The ghost's name was Euphrosyne.

Madame Sophie listened to Euphrosyne's story with sympathy and candidly shared her own sad tale. When she finished, Euphrosyne cried out in great anger. "Oh, that so many centuries have passed and still women are excluded from the realm that should be ours by birthright!" she lamented, and Madame Sophie's anger at this injustice–long tamped down and strictly ignored–was brought again to light.

Then Euphrosyne lingered, and when she spoke again, she told Madame Sophie of a plan.

It was a thing that had never happened before, could not possibly have been imagined to happen–it was not even to be thought of! And yet, it had happened, and there was no denying it:

There was a ghost haunting the Académie des Sciences.

It wandered through the halls, moaning and wailing. It interrupted lectures, and whispered nonsense into the ears of the boys taking exams. It moved notes and–some said–scribbled incorrect numbers into equations. The senior scientists ranted and raved and complained, and set the junior scientists to work: never mind their other research, their task now was to find a way to exorcise the ghost.

Madame Sophie came along one day, and offered her services. "For I am well-skilled in languages and can listen to ghosts. Let me help you."

"No, no, no!" the scientists said. "We shall do this, for we are scientists. We do not need the assistance of a woman!

This problem can only be solved with science, and thus it is only men who can solve it."

And Madame Sophie let herself be persuaded to leave.

The junior scientists worked day and night, and still they found no way to remove the ghost. The ghost developed a particularly annoying habit of peering over the shoulders of the men, the scientists, as they read their books and measured their flasks and wrote in their journals, so that no one could concentrate on anything. Eventually the senior scientists left their pet projects to gather dust, to work alongside the junior scientists, and they wrote to the king begging money, for everyone knows the best science requires both money and patronage.

Again Madame Sophie came, and again she offered to speak to the ghost. "For perhaps I may have luck where you have not yet," she said.

"Luck!" the scientists replied. "Science is not a matter of luck! It is a matter of, well, science! Fact, and reason, and experiment! We shall do this on our own!"

But they were still unable. They spoke every language they knew, and even tried some they did not know, and still they could not find out what it was the ghost desired. The scientists applied to the king for more money, and the king gave it them, and scientists came from all over the country and still they could not rid themselves of the ghost.

One day, a junior scientist thought of how Madame Sophie had twice come to offer her help and twice been turned away. This junior scientist–his name was Jean–thought how silly it was that they were professing to avail themselves of all available resources, and yet they continually refused Madame Sophie. And he thought again how strange it was, what all the other scientists said, that only men could be scientists. This, Jean thought, was itself a claim to be tested and proved by science itself, and he had an uncomfortable suspicion that should he or any of the other scientists do so, they would not be pleased with what they found.

Why should women not be scientists? There was no reason in science that he could think of. So Jean, who had never thought of himself as a daring sort of fellow until this day, confronted the senior scientists and put forth his case and pleaded it until at last they agreed to consider it: for the king had said he had no more money to give them, and they were at their wit's end.

"Madame Sophie," they begged her, "Please come. With all of our money and all of our learning, we cannot rid ourselves of this ghost."

And then Madame Sophie's eyes sparkled, and she hid her smile. "But you said quite clearly that only science can rid you of your ghost. What can I offer you? For I am but a woman, and women cannot be scientists."

Then Claude, the most senior of the scientists, hung his head and lowered his eyes and said that if she could rid them of the ghost, then by reason's dictates she must be a scientist, and would be offered as reward admittance into the Académie des Sciences with full rights and responsibilities.

Madame Sophie accepted the bargain, and accompanied Claude and Jean and the others to the Académie. There she listened to Euphrosyne, and Euphrosyne said that she would leave off haunting the scientists and let them return to their work on one condition: that she too be granted leave to finally be accounted as a scientist, and to take up a place alongside Madame Sophie in the Académie.

The scientists turned to one another and shrugged their shoulders, and Jean offered that they might as well be hung for a sheep as for a lamb. So Claude put his hands out in resignation and honored his promise that Madame Sophie be admitted to the Académie and accounted as a scientist, for she had indeed done as had been asked of her. And at the same time, Euphrosyne was enrolled beside her.

The Chenoo

Edward Ahern

This is a retelling of a tale from The Algonquin Legends of New England by Charles G. Leland. The book was published in 1884, but the story is much older. Lewis Brooks, a Micmac Indian, heard the story from his grandfather, Samuel Paul, sometime before 1843. No one knows how much older than that the story really is.

Of the old time, a Micmac Indian went with his wife one autumn far away in the northwest to hunt. They found a good place to pass the winter, and built a wigwam. The man hunted and brought home game. The woman dressed and dried the meat.

One winter afternoon, while the woman foraged through the snow to gather wood, she heard rustling in the bushes. She looked up and saw something worse than she had ever feared.

A haggard old man with wolf eyes stared at her, his face a mix of devil and beast. His shoulders and lips were gnawed away, as if he had been so hungry he had begun to eat himself. He carried a bundle on his back.

The woman knew about the Chenoos, beings from the far, icy north, both devil and cannibal. She knew this was one of them.

Dire need sometimes gives one quick wit. The woman, despite her fear, ran up to the Chenoo and pretended surprise and joy. "My dear father, how glad my heart is. Where have you been for so long?"

The Chenoo was amazed. He expected screams and prayers. In silence he let himself be led into the wigwam. The wise woman looked at his ragged clothes and dirty body.

"Here father," she said. "Here are clothes of my husband. Dress yourself and be cleaned."

The Chenoo looked surly, but kept quiet. It was a new thing to him. The woman got up and went out to gather more branches. The Chenoo stood up and followed her. *Now*, she thought, *my death is here. Now he will kill and eat me.*

The Chenoo stood in front of her. "Give me the axe," he said. She handed him the axe, and he began to chop down trees. Man never saw such chopping. Great pines fell on one side and the other like summer saplings. The branches were hewed and split as if by a great tempest.

"*Noo, tabeagul boosoogul!*" the woman cried. "My father, that is enough!" The Chenoo handed her the axe and, in grim silence, walked back into the wigwam and sat down. The woman gathered wood and returned to the wigwam, sitting in silence across from the Chenoo.

Then she heard her husband coming through the snow. "Rest here my father," she said. She ran out and told her husband what she had done. He thought it well. The husband went into the wigwam. "*N'chilch*," he said kindly, "my father in law, where have you so long been?"

The Chenoo stared in amazement. As the husband told of the many years he and the woman had been together, the Chenoo's fierce face grew gentler. He sat for the meal, but hardly touched the food they offered him. The Chenoo lay down to sleep, but the fire was too warm. "Put a screen in front of me," he said. The Chenoo was from the ice and could not endure heat.

For three days, the Chenoo rested in the wigwam, sullen and grim, hardly eating. Then he changed. "Woman," he asked, "do you have tallow?"

"Yes my father," the woman replied. "We have much deer fat."

The Chenoo filled a large kettle with tallow. He put the kettle on the fire. When the tallow was scalding hot, he drank it all in one swallow. He grew pale. He became sick. He cast up every kind of horrible thing he had eaten, terrible to see and smell. He lay down and slept. When he woke, he asked for food and ate much. From that time on, he was good to them. They feared him no more. He now seemed as an old man.

They lived on dried meat such as the Micmacs prepare. The Chenoo grew tired of it. "*N'toos*-my daughter-, have you no -*pela weoos*--fresh meat?"

"No, my father," she replied.

When the husband returned, the Chenoo saw black mud on his snowshoes.

"Son-in-law, is there a spring near?"

"Half a day's trek away."

"We will go there tomorrow," said the Chenoo.

They went early the next morning. The husband ran very quickly in snowshoes. But the Chenoo, who seemed wasted and worn, ran in snowshoes ahead of the wind. They came to the spring, the snow melted around it, the fringe flat and green.

The Chenoo stripped out of his clothes and began a magic dance. The spring water began to foam and rise and fall, as if something below were heaving along with the steps and the song. The head of a huge -*Taktalok*-lizard rose above the surface. The Chenoo killed it with a chop of his hatchet. He dragged the lizard out of the spring and began to dance again. A second lizard, a female, stuck her head above the surface and was killed. She was smaller than the first, but still heavy as an elk.

"How is this?" asked the husband.

"They were only small spring lizards, son-in-law, but I have conjured them into monsters."

The Chenoo dressed the game and cut it up. He took the head, feet and tails and threw them back into the spring. "These will grow again into many lizards," he said.

The dressed meat looked like bear. The Chenoo bound the meat together with withes of willow twigs and put the load on his shoulders. Then he began to run before the wind, his load as nothing.

The husband was the greatest runner in the region, but he lagged far behind. "You cannot go fast enough," said the Chenoo, "the sun is setting, the red will be black soon. Get on my back. Brace your feet. Duck your head low so you will not be knocked off by branches."

The Chenoo -*nebe sokano'u'jal samastukteskugulchel wegwasumug wegul-*, ran ahead of the wind, bushes whistling as they flew past them. They reached the wigwam before sunset. The wife was afraid to prepare such meat, but the husband persuaded her. It tasted of bear meat.

Spring came. The Chenoo told them that his enemy, a Chenoo woman, was coming from the north to kill him. This woman Chenoo, he said, was more mad and cruel than he had been. The man and his wife must hide, for even the war-whoops of a female Chenoo might kill them.

The Chenoo sent the woman for the bundle which he had brought with him and which had been hanging untouched on a tree bough. He took out two horns, golden bright, of the -*chepitchcalm-,* a dragon. One horn had two tines, the other was straight. He gave the straight horn to the husband.

"Only these," he told the husband, "will kill the Chenoo. If you hear me call for help, then run to me with the horn, for you may be able to save me."

Three days passed. The Chenoo was fierce and bold. He sat and listened, but had no fear. Then, far away, from the icy north, he heard the awful scream, like nothing else that lived. The husband and wife hid in a deep hole they had dug.

The battle began with the war-whoops of the two Chenoos. They made magic and grew to the size of hills. As they fought, thick pines were torn up out of ground, and boulders crashed into boulders.

Then the husband heard the old man Chenoo cry out, "*N'loosook! Choogooye! Abog unumoee!* Son-in-law, come help me!"

The husband ran into the fight. The female Chenoo was holding old man Chenoo down, stabbing at his ear with her dragon's horn. She mocked him, "You have no son-in-law to help you. I will take your life and eat your liver."

The husband stood next to the struggling Chenoos, so small he was not noticed. "Now," said old man Chenoo, "jab the horn into her ear."

The husband struck hard, and the horn pierced her ear. As soon as the horn entered the ear, it lengthened and shot through her head, coming out the other ear like a long pole. The end of the horn touched ground and sprouted strong roots. The other end of the horn grew from the husband's hand and coiled itself around a massive tree.

Old man Chenoo and the husband began to kill the female Chenoo. She had shrunk to her normal size, but the killing was long, weary work. They must chop her body into bits and burn every piece completely, otherwise a new Chenoo, worse than the first, would grow from any overlooked fragment. The hardest task of all was to melt and burn her heart. It was harder than ice, harder than ice as ice is harder than water, as ice is colder than fire.

At last they were done.

Spring continued. The winter snows ran down the rivers to the sea, the ice and snow on the inland hills seeking the shore. The Chenoo was becoming as a man, his soul also softening and melting.

The husband and his wife knew it was time to leave. They prepared their birch bark canoe, but for the old man Chenoo they made a canoe of moose skins. In his canoe they put their venison and skins. The old man did not lead, but merely followed the couple in his canoe, down into the sunshine of a wide lake. But he was not fond of the sunshine.

When they came to the outlet river the old man Chenoo said that they should tow his canoe and that he would travel downstream through the woods. They told the old man where they meant to camp that night, and he started out on foot, through dense brush, over hills and rocks, a much harder, longer trip.

Husband and wife sailed down river with the spring floods, headlong through rapids. But when they came to the point where they meant to camp they saw smoke already rising from among the trees. After landing they found old man Chenoo sleeping away from the fire which he had built for the two of them.

This was repeated for several days, moving further south into a warmer valley. But as they traveled a change came over the old man. He was of the north. Ice and snow had no effect on him, but he could not abide the soft airs of summer.

The old man grew weaker and weaker. When husband and wife reached their village, the old man had to be carried like a small child.

Thoughtful Young

His face was no longer fierce, His wounds had healed. He no longer grinned wildly. He had become gentle. He was as their father. As he was dying. The Chenoo cried for the first and last time as a man.

The Little Holly

Amy Hammack Turner

From the time she was just a seedling, the little holly admired the bright red berries of the older female hollies. She knew in her heartwood that she would have berries when she matured.

With this knowledge, she grew happily among her siblings, cousins, and friends, all of whom clustered companionably beneath the taller trees reaching towards the life-giving sky. The poplars stood regally straight, the oaks bore the wisdom of their years on their boughs, and the hickories graciously distributed their nuts to the deer, squirrels, rabbits, and birds.

The brief lives of the animals, punctuated by vivid fears and desires, intertwined with the trees' slower, calmer progression through the seasons.

Each spring, some of the young hollies flowered for the first time. Some flaunted female flowers, with bountiful green centers that would ripen into berries. Others produced male flowers, the four white petals surrounding a dark, diminutive center from which four yellow-tipped stamens thrust out brashly. Bees tickled the stamens as they gathered nectar and carried pollen to the pistils of the female hollies. The newly mature trees rejoiced in their attractiveness to the bees, in the uniting of pollen and ovules, in the promise of berries and seedlings to come.

As the flowering of the redbud trees heralded her fifth spring, the little holly dreamed of her first flowering. Surely, she had grown enough to join the older trees in their glad joining. She envisioned her dainty white flowers luring bees to their center and trembled at the thought of her stigma gathering pollen from the insects' hairy bodies.

But when the long-awaited blossoms finally appeared, the holly's sap froze as she realized that her flowers were male. With no stigma, no ovaries, they felt like insects gnawing on her newest, most tender shoots. Despair permeated her fine-grained wood as bees carried her pollen to the fertile green centers of female flowers.

Betrayed by her own anatomy, she found no solace in the fact that both males and females were necessary for her species to continue. If she could not be a female holly, why had she not sprouted as one of the trees that have both male and female parts? She did not envy the oaks, poplars and hickories for their place in the canopy, but all the dogwoods bore beautiful berries.

For three years, she could put little energy into pulling nutrients from the earth, and barely grew. One fall, a chickadee brought hope in a whistled story. In winter, he sang, Father Christmas wandered the woods and sometimes granted wishes. His route varied every year. This year, perhaps, he would pass this way.

The little holly did not see Father Christmas that year or the next, but hope flowed now in her sap. Her kind lived a hundred years or more. She could wait decades for her wish to be granted. As she had as a seedling, she savored the touch of the wind, the rain, and the sunlight.

It was a moonlit night when Father Christmas came; a solemn old man robed in black, bent under the weight of a large sack. He paused before the holly and understood her wish.

"Such a change is not easy," he said. "I can grant you just one season, and when you die, you will not come back as a new seedling."

The little holly did not hesitate. The trees all believed that they would sprout again, but none remembered a previous life. It meant nothing to her that she might be a female in many future lives. She wanted berries in this life, if only for one season. "Yes, yes!" her soul sang out.

"This spring, you will flower as a female," Father Christmas said. His face paled. The holly sensed he, too, had paid a price for the gift.

In the spring, the little holly raised her ovaries, encircled by delicate white petals, joyously toward the sun. In the fall, the flowers transformed into glorious red berries. Birds fluttered in her branches and carried her fruit out into the forest so that her seedlings could flourish far from her roots.

oOo

"Why don't people use hollies for Christmas trees?" Alicia asked. "There's the song about decking the halls, but that's just with boughs."

Her mother shrugged. "Just custom," she answered.

"Can we have a holly this Christmas? The woods are full of them. I think it would be prettier than a prickly cedar. It would come pre-decorated with berries."

"If you want to cut down a holly and haul it in, go ahead," her mother said.

"I'll decorate it while the little ones are still in daycare," Alicia said. "They'll be so surprised when they get home." At age twelve, she enjoyed having the house to herself after school and welcoming her mother and her little brother and sister home from work and daycare.

Immediately after school the next day, Alicia went out into the woods that were part of the property that her mother had inherited from her parents. She loved to walk here and knew where to find hollies. She took her time selecting the right tree, one that would almost touch the living room ceiling, had regular branches that would look good from all angles, and most importantly bore bright, abundant berries.

As she positioned the saw on the little holly's trunk, she hesitated for a moment. It was a pity to cut such a beautiful tree. Maybe she should choose a tree that needed love, as Charlie Brown did in the Christmas special. She looked at her watch. If she wanted to decorate the tree before her mother brought the children home, she needed to hurry. The teeth of the saw bit into the smooth gray bark. Did it hurt a tree to be cut down?

oOo

Hannah and Josh rushed into the living room and knelt under the Christmas tree, their bright eyes reflecting the colored lights. Alicia had hung paper snowflakes and tinsel icicles, and little red bird figurines perched on the branches.

"It's beautiful," Mom said, smiling. She always looked so tired after work.

The children's voices reminded the little holly of birdsong, and their trilling laughter recalled the chatter of squirrels. She was terrified when the girl had cut her down and dragged her into this strange place. Now the girl and her mother lay colorful presents beneath the little holly, as if she embodied a goddess. Maybe Father Christmas planned this as part of his gift. She knew she wouldn't live long cut off from the earth and nourished only by a small dish of water and the indirect light of the sun. However, in the forest, all her berries would soon have been eaten, and she didn't want to return to a fruitless life. She thought it better to have the human family gathered around her in admiration as she ended her one brief season as a mother.

The holly was dry and weak when the girl removed her decorations, took her out to a field, and threw her onto a pile of dead branches. She enjoyed being under the sky again as her sap dried, and her thoughts faded. As if from a great distance, she sensed winter giving way to spring.

She awoke to the heat and crackle of fire. She burned along with the dry branches that she had lain with for months. Once again, the girl and her siblings accompanied her, their faces glowing in the light of the bonfire. As the little holly's wood crumbled into ashes, her spirit rose in smoke toward the constant stars. Dispersing into the warm air, she became part of the spring, part of the coming summer. Fragments of her being would diffuse into the pores of the leaves of her kindred trees. Losing her individuality, becoming part of the continual birthing of new life, she knew she would be female forever.

Brick by Brick

Allan Rousselle

So, I ate a brick house the other day.

It was the third house on my list of three. The first one was made of straw, and I made short business of *that* one, let me tell you. The second wasn't quite as easy as the first, but I still did okay. I just huffed and I puffed until I made my way to the chewy center and enjoyed a deeelicious meal.

The third one, though. That was a problem. No matter how much I huffed and I puffed, it just wasn't coming down. No siree, Bob.

I asked the tasty little morsel inside to let me in, but he just went on and on about his facial hair and said, "Not gonna happen."

You'd think that if you asked somebody nice and pleasant-like to let you in to eat them, they'd be more than happy to open their door wide open and let you do what you're going to do anyway.

But no, this little piggy stayed home, and he wasn't letting me in.

So I said, "Look, pal, if'n you don't let me in, I'm gonna huff and puff," thinking that maybe that would change his mind. But it didn't, so I did, and like I said before, huffing and puffing at brick houses is about as effective as spitting on a fish.

Now the guy inside starts singing this song about how nobody's afraid of big bad me, which is just getting me madder and madder. I just ate two of his kin in their flimsy little shacks and he's thumbing his hoof at me with a big ol' "Neener, neener."

That just ain't right.

So I figure, if he ain't gonna let me in, I can just wait out here 'til he comes out. You see, while he's on my list to eat and all, it's not like I was starving just yet. I mean, after all,

I'd just had a couple of deeelicious meals, and I could handle a little break between courses, if you catch my meaning.

The guy inside, a pig by the name of Arnold— and no, I don't mean Roseanne Arnold— was clever enough to build a brick house without even having opposable hooves, which musta been quite a trick, if you ask me, and I'm pretty sure he knew a brick house would stand up to huffing and puffing, but he only built it with one door.

You might say this was a bit of a mistake, strategic-wise, because it meant if'n I wanted to wait him out, I only had to wait just outside that one door. It also meant if'n I wanted to lock him in, well, there was just one point of egress, as my cousin Petunia used to say, that needed blocking.

So I waited outside that one door, but he wasn't coming out.

"Come out, come out, wherever you are," I said, but he just kept singing inside that brick house of his about how he'd been to market and well, next thing you know, I smell roast beef coming from inside the house.

There was smoke coming from the chimney. He was cooking his roast beef on a fire in his fireplace, and that's what made me realize that I coulda just jumped up on the roof and climbed down and gotten in that way. No huffing or puffing required.

But now it was too late, because he was cooking hisself some dinner and going down the chimney would be mighty hot.

But that gave me an idea on how I might be able to get him to come out to me instead of making me go in to get him.

I kept an eye on that one point of egress, as my uncle Wilbur would call it, while I went to where the shack next door used to be and picked up the sticks and piled them up around the outside of the brick house.

Then I pulled out my box of matches and got a match and tried to light one of the sticks and boy, if you think it's hard to light a brick on fire without kindling, I'm here to tell you thick old sticks ain't much better when all you got is them little Ohio blue-tip matches.

But the pig in the poke was still singing about not being afraid of big bad me and by the sounds and the smells he

44

was still enjoying his roast beef so I went over to where the other shack used to be, the straw one just two spots over, and I got a bunch of the straw and piled that up in and around the sticks.

This time when I pulled out a match and lit it, well, that straw caught fire real nice-like.

Oh, and if you're wondering how a wolf with no opposable paws can light a match, I'll remind you that these were those blue-tip matches, the kind you can light with your teeth.

So the straw caught on fire, but just in that one area, so I huffed and I puffed like they taught us in cub scouts and once the sticks caught on fire, I took one and used it to light up the kindling all around the brick house.

Well, I stood back and watched that front door, but soon I noticed a great big old plume of smoke rising out of the chimney, which got me to thinking maybe my next meal had just doused the fire he had in his fireplace.

Sure enough, before too long, he pops up out of the chimney and he says for me to cut it out, it's getting all hot in his house. All them sticks are burning real nice by this time.

And I says, no, I'm not going to stop, and in fact I trot next door to get some more sticks and I drop them on the fire.

Well, that just makes him mad, boy I'll tell you, and he disappears again and then pops up with a hammer and he whacks one of the bricks from his chimney loose and he throws it at me.

Yessiree, Bob, that's what he did, and you know what I did? Well, I saw I was breaking his will, so I decided to keep pressing my advantage in this little psychological duel we was playing out. I caught that hurling brick right between my teeth, I did, and I chomped and I chewed and I swallowed that sucker and just grinned up at him with the meanest, nastiest, ugliest grin I knew how to grin.

Oh, man, you shoulda seen the look of fear in his eyes. Well, now he starts to panic-like, and he whacks at them bricks in his chimney and throws them down at me, and I show him I ain't gonna stop, and I just keeps chomping and chewing and eating and grinning.

And as he worked his way down the house, tearing it apart brick by brick and tossing them at me, the fire around his house died down, too, until there was nothing left but the concrete foundation, the front door, and the smoldering remains of my fire going around the outside.

Well, all that plus his furniture, which was really quite lovely.

So now there wasn't no house for me to even huff and puff down, except for the door and the foundation, and you can't very well blow down a foundation. But he's just standing inside there, looking out at me through where there used to be bricks, and I'm just staring back at him, thinking that this time he's just *got* to open the front door and come out.

But then I realized something. I wasn't hungry no more. It wouldn't matter if he came out or not, because I just flat out lost my appetite.

So I nod to the pig once-like, and he nods to me once-like, and I saunter on my way and leave him standing there on his smoldering foundation with the one big door sticking up and that exquisite furniture— I'll have to ask him where he got it, someday—and saved that particular meal for another day, I guess.

But that's all by way of saying, my little cubs, that if you're hungry enough to eat a house, you don't eat it all at once.

You eat it one brick at a time.

Cinderfeller

Liz Tuckwell

There was once a rich merchant called Anna who lived in a fine mansion. She thought her husband beautiful and her little boy, Soren, lovely.

They were kind generous people so they adopted a little girl orphan to be a sister for him. Jerymene's green eyes were the same shade as the buttons on her coat that she arrived in, so they nicknamed her, "Buttons." They were all very happy.

But then, alas, tragedy struck. Her husband died in a plague, and Anna and her children were left alone. Anna mourned her dead husband for some time, but well-meaning friends told her she was being selfish and should think of a new father for her little son and daughter.

Anna roused herself from her grief and soon met a poor widower who had recently come to live in their city. His name was Frederick Stone.

"And he has sons of his own," said Anna, justifying the decision to herself, "so the marriage will provide extra playmates for my son and daughter."

While the widower had a beautiful face, his smile never reached his eyes. She put his aside for the children, his in need of a mother, hers in need of a father.

They were married, and Frederick and his sons came to live in the Anna's large mansion. Flounce, the elder son, was monstrously fat and hairy. Grizzle, the younger, was horribly skinny. His hair so sparse, he bore a bald patch despite his young age.

These quirks in appearance didn't matter, but the boys were lazy, cruel, and selfish.

The stepfather doted on them both and instantly disliked Soren and Buttons. It was perhaps, because Anna spent money on them, and not just himself and his sons. Or perhaps Soren's large blue eyes and long golden hair annoyed him.

For a time, all was well. However, Anna's new husband had tastes his previous poverty had not allowed, or were perhaps the cause of it. Whatever the reason, Anna found herself pushed to make even more money and went abroad to pursue more profitable business ventures.

Disaster struck.

Frederick received news, rather casually, that she had drowned.

Despite the lack of income, Frederick carried on with his extravagant ways. To economize, he gradually rid the mansion of servants, pocketing their wages for his own use.

Bereft of their mother, Soren and Buttons found solace in talking about her and remembering the good times. Then Frederick sent Buttons back to the orphanage.

Soren cried great tears and clung to her until the orphanage mistress pulled her from his arms.

"Such a fuss about nothing," their stepfather said.

As the servants left, Soren was given their chores. Finally, there were no servants left, and he did all the cleaning, cooking, and washing. His lazy stepbrothers lounged about the house all day when they weren't going out to play dice with their friends.

Soren was often besmirched with the ashes he cleaned from the stoves each morning and had no time to clean them off until the end of each long day. His nasty stepbrothers nicknamed him "Cinderfeller," because of his dirty face and clothes. This nickname stuck, and soon, he was always called that, his real name forgotten.

Cinderfeller was very lonely, and the highlight of his life were the odd visits that Buttons made. She'd been lucky and was chosen to work at the palace. She would visit, bringing cakes and chocolate and gossip. Buttons sang the praises of the princess; how handsome and clever and kind she was. Sadly, these occasions were rare, as they kept Buttons very busy.

Cinderfeller grew up like that, without any time for his own pursuits or friends or recreation, the queen announced a grand ball. She invited all the beautiful young gentlemen of the queendom so Princess Charming, the heir to the throne, could choose a bridegroom. She had rejected all the foreign princes selected for her and declared she would marry only her own choice.

A messenger rode to Centerfielder's house and presented a bundle of envelopes embossed with the royal crest to the cruel stepfather. Frederick and his sons were very excited when they opened the envelopes. Inside were the royal invitations, one for Frederick, one for Flounce, and one for Grizzle.

"We shall go to the ball, my darlings, and the princess will surely choose one of you to marry," pronounced Frederick.

"Is there one for me?" asked Cinderfeller.

"Don't be ridiculous," scoffed his cruel stepfather. "Who would want you at the ball with your dirty face and patched clothes? Be off with you, the chamber pots need cleaning."

Once Cinderfeller was gone, Frederick retrieved the envelope addressed to Soren Worthing he had hidden in a book and put it into the fire.

Cinderfeller wept once he was back in the kitchen. He would have liked very much to wear a fine suit and go to a ball, but everyone had forgotten him. Buttons interrupted his crying.

"Don't cry, Soren, see, I've brought you an invitation."

Buttons pulled out a large white card embossed with gold writing. Cinderfeller gasped.

"I sneaked one out from the pile for you and wrote your name on it," Buttons said. "I'm the princess's page and helped send out the invitations."

Cinderfeller hugged her, which Buttons allowed even though she would have to brush her uniform later. Buttons had even brought a second-hand, bright red suit and worn-out shoes for him to wear.

Cinderfeller added sequins he'd filched from his stepbrothers to the lapels of the jacket and decorated each shoe with a rose.

The afternoon before the ball Centerfielder waxed Flounce's moustache. He washed and combed out Grizzle's towering, plum-coloured wig that matched his suit and hid his balding pate. He polished the shoes of all three gentlemen. Finally, he helped them into their clothes.

When they had left to meet the rented carriage, for his mother's carriage had been long sold, he scampered upstairs. He changed into his suit and brushed his golden hair. Then he went down the back steps and out the kitchen door. But as Cinderfeller emerged from the alley that ran alongside the house, he was horrified to see his stepfather and stepbrothers still waiting for their coach. They turned and saw him.

As one, they rushed on him. Frederick plucked the invitation out of his hand and tore it in two. Flounce pulled so hard at one sleeve that it tore off and made the jacket unwearable. Grizzle grabbed Cinderfeller's foot, pulled off a shoe, and tossed it out into the street where the arriving coach ran it over.

Laughing and chortling, they all got into the coach, but not without squabbling about who would sit where, and drove off.

Cinderfeller stood in the street, still as a statue, while one tear coursed down his cheek. Then he heard a gentle voice he had never heard before.

"Dear me, what is this? Why are you crying?"

A beautiful gentleman stood there, wearing a powdered wig and a gleaming pink silk dress. A sparkling tiara crowned his luxuriant hair, and he carried a wand.

Cinderfeller bowed. "If you please sir, I'm crying because I want to go to the ball but now, I have nothing to wear." Cinderfeller gazed dismally after the coach in the distance.

"I must apologise, I have been much delayed, but never mind. "It's not too late," the beautiful gentleman said.

"Too late for what?" asked Cinderfeller.

"Why, for you to go to the ball!'"

Cinderfeller laughed. "I don't know who you are, but thank you for cheering me up. But I must return to my chores."

"Don't you know who I am? I'm your Fairy Godfather Dominic, dear child."

Cinderfeller stared at him. "Can this be true?"

"Of course, it's true. Now, let's go into the garden. Make haste, for there is much to do."

Once in the back garden, Dominic surveyed the area and nodded. "This will do nicely."

With a wave of his wand, he transformed four scrawny rats into magnificent white horses. Then a plump duck was turned into a plump coach woman, and two green lizards transformed into footwomen. Next, he turned his attention to a large pumpkin, and it became a gleaming golden coach.

"Get in," Dominic told Cinderfeller. "We haven't any time to waste."

"But how can I go, dressed like this?' cried Cinderfeller. He indicated his jacket with only one sleeve and his one shoe.

His fairy godfather clicked his tongue. "I was forgetting," he admitted. He waved his wand once more. "Don't lose the boots," he said, "they're specially made to fit only you."

"Boots?"

Cinderfeller gazed down in astonishment at a suit of dazzling silver covered with pearls. On his feet were ermine boots.

"Too much," said Dominic. He waved his wand again and only the lapels and cuffs of the jacket were covered in pearls. "Perhaps in gold?" mused his fairy godfather. He raised his wand again.

Cinderfeller stamped his foot. "I'll be late for the ball!"

"Oh, very well." His fairy godfather lowered his wand. "Now, remember, Soren, you must leave the ball on time, for on the stroke of midnight everything will return to its normal state of being. Oh, and take this."

He thrust the invitation to the ball, miraculously restored to pristine condition, into Cinderfeller's hands.

Cinderfeller eagerly assured his fairy godfather he would remember the warning, and Cinderfeller went off in the golden coach.

Cinderfeller was one of the last people to arrive at the ball. The large, splendidly uniformed woman at the top of the long flight of stairs leading down to the ballroom, asked what his name was.

"Er.. mm nnn name..." stammered Cinderfeller.

Before he could finish the sentence, she read the invitation and bellowed out, "Prince Ermine."

Everyone looked up. The princess not only looked up, but kept on staring. It was love at first sight. She rushed up to him after he had descended the stairs and asked him to dance. They danced the night away, and the princess only had eyes for him. Cinderfeller was equally entranced by her.

The other young men in the ballroom grumbled. None were louder or more vociferous than Flounce and Grizzle. The queen smiled to see her daughter so enthralled. She wondered which queendom Prince Ermine came from.

Cinderfeller had never been so happy in his life as he whirled around the dance floor with the princess. He happened to look up at the huge, ornate clock and saw to his shock that it was ten to twelve. He recalled his fairy godfather's words. "You must leave the ball on the stroke of midnight for then everything will return to its normal state of being."

Cinderfeller pulled himself away from the princess and ran across the ballroom, pushing dancers out of the way. He dashed up the stairs. Cinderfeller knew he wouldn't have time to get back to his home in the coach, so he ran as fast as he could. But as he ran, one of his boots worked loose, and he stumbled. He kicked off the boot and ran on.

Princess Charming stood stock still for a moment, and then ran after the enchanting stranger. By the time the princess reached the courtyard, she found not Prince Ermine, but one furry boot. She clutched this to her heart. Princess Charming declared to her mother, "Whomsoever this boot fits, I shall marry!"

They issued the proclamation the very next day, and all the young gentlemen of the land were very excited. They assumed the princess would only try the boot on the feet of gentlemen. There was great surprise when Princess Charming made it clear that she would try the boot on the foot of every young man, high or low.

The ugly stepbrothers and the cruel stepfather were all of a tizzy at their mansion.

"This is your chance," declared the cruel stepfather, "seize it with both hands."

"Or feet," said Grizzle and sniggered. He got cuffed for his wit.

Eventually, the princess and her guards came to the house of Cinderfeller. Buttons was included in her retinue. The cruel stepfather had taken the precaution of locking Cinderfeller in the cellar.

Buttons took the fur boot off the cushion it was resting on and proffered it to Flounce. First, Flounce sat down and tried to put on the boot, but his foot was too big and his calves too wide. Flounce stood up to complain, and Grizzle pushed his brother out of the way. He sat down and did get his foot inside, but it was clear that the boot was far too big for him. It flopped on the end of his leg.

Buttons did her best not to laugh.

Frederick bit his lip with anger and frustration until drops of blood appeared.

"Are these the only young men in the house?" Princess Charming asked.

"Oh yes," Frederick assured her. "No one else."

"She's lying, Your Highness," Buttons told the princess. "There's a young boy in the kitchen who does all the work."

"Her Highness couldn't possibly be interested in that ragamuffin," said the cruel stepfather.

"Let him be brought," the princess ordered. Secretly, she agreed with Frederick, but she was a fair woman and always kept her promises.

Buttons and the guards went into the kitchen and she called out his name. They heard his faint cry and unlocked the door. Cinderfeller emerged from the cellar. They brought him to the drawing room. Princess Charming at once saw how beautiful he was, even under the grime and rags. Was this her Prince Ermine?

"Please try on the boot," she said.

Cinderfeller blushed and walked over to where Buttons knelt. He slipped out of his worn-out slippers and put his foot into the boot. It fit perfectly.

"No!" howled Frederick and hurled himself across the room to tear off the boot.

The guards pulled him away.

"It's you," breathed the princess.

Cinderfeller smiled. "I didn't think you'd find me," he said.

"This is my bridegroom," the princess announced. She turned to the guards. "Put those creatures in jail for three days for lying to their princess."

She swept Cinderfeller out of the house as the cruel stepfather and the ugly stepbrothers gaped in amazement. Then they began to wail.

Soren and his princess married and lived happily ever after.

Frederick was given a job as a palace laundry worker, and Flounce and Grizzle jobs as scullery workers. Buttons was promoted to major-domo of the royal household. She kept a strict watch on them to make sure they worked hard all day long and were given the worst jobs to do.

And no one ever called Soren "Cinderfeller" again.

Just Enough

Rebecca van den Ham

Once there was an orphan boy called Tripp. He was all alone in the world. He wore tattered rags, his only possessions. He spent his days searching out odd jobs and his nights curled in a doorway or stable.

One day he thought, *This town is not the whole world. Perhaps I will be better off somewhere else.*

So he set out to seek his fortune.

Tripp traveled for several days and came one night to a snug cottage in the middle of a dense wood. Light blazed from within, so he knocked on the door, hoping the owner would spare a bit of old bread in exchange for his labor. An old woman with soft eyes and a gentle smile opened the door.

"I was just sitting down to a lonely supper," she said. "Will you join me?"

"Please, mother, let me work for it," said Tripp.

"Very well," she said. "I am Goodwife Hannah. In the morning, you may chop wood for me."

Gladly Tripp accepted and sat down at Hannah's table. Over the meal he told her of his dreams and travels.

"I don't have much to offer," she said when he had finished. "I'm just a poor widow. But stay here tonight before you continue on your way."

Tripp agreed and curled up in a warm bed. The next morning after the wood was chopped, Hannah fed him again and packed food for him to take along. He thanked her and prepared to leave.

"Take this as well, my dear." She offered him a small, brown paper package. "This is something my grandmother gave me when I was just a girl. I had hoped to pass it on to a child or grandchild of my own, but that was not to be. I enjoyed your company, Tripp, so I want you to have it.

Whenever you are in need, use this and it will be just enough."

"Tripp thanked her again and set off. When he came to the far edge of the wood, he stopped to rest and opened the package. Inside he found a chunky, white, china teacup. It looked quite ordinary. Wondering, he put it away and walked on.

"Soon he came to a wide, slow-flowing river with no bridge in sight. Looking around, he saw an old weathered rowboat sitting on the bank. Tripp heaved the boat into the water and began to row. But the wood was dry and he quickly spotted a leak. Water trickled, then poured in, freezing his feet. By the time he was midway across, inches of water covered the boat's bottom.

"Tugging harder at the oars, he thought, *This river is deep and I can't swim!*

"Suddenly Tripp thought of the teacup. He dug it out and held it hopefully. Nothing happened. Growing desperate, he did the first logical thing that came to mind: He began to bail.

"After frantically scooping out water, Tripp glanced down into the boat. The water was reduced to puddles. Tripp was amazed. *There must be less water than I thought.*

He began to row again. The boat continued to leak, but the cup was just enough to keep the water out until he reached the opposite shore. He carefully packed up the teacup and went on his way.

Tripp tried to make his food last, but it soon ran out. He was overjoyed to see a wild berry bush growing near the road. For lack of a basket, he took out the teacup and picked berries into it.

"He found only a few berries on the bush, barely enough to fill the cup. Disappointed, Tripp sat down to eat his meager meal. He slowly put berry after berry into his mouth, trying to savor each one, not dwelling on their diminishing number. He had a foggy notion that he must have eaten far more than he had picked. Just as he was beginning to feel full, he reached into the cup to find that it was empty.

"How about that," he said aloud. "Just enough."

"Tripp lay down under a shady tree near the berry bush and fell asleep with the teacup cradled in his hands. He was rattled awake by the sound of pounding hooves. Scrambling to his feet, cup still in hand, Tripp beheld a horse and rider nearly upon him.

The rider, seeing him, hastily reined his impatient stallion to a halt in front of Tripp. The richly dressed man surveyed Tripp, then tossed a couple of golden coins expertly into the teacup.

"Always glad to help the poor," said the man before spurring his horse and galloping away.

Tripp gazed at the coins, then gathered his pack and headed for the nearest town. *No more rags*, he said to himself.

He bought strong boots, a warm cloak, and clothes made of plain, sturdy cloth. Each time he looked in the cup, he found one more gold coin.

Next, he desired a belt of tooled leather that would be the finishing touch for his new outfit. He reached into the teacup for another coin but found it empty.

Now I understand, he thought. *I don't need that belt. What I have is just enough.*

As he curled up on the ground to sleep that night, he began to think about a soft, warm bed. The next morning, he started back the way he had come.

Goodwife Hannah opened her door with a look of surprise. "Why Tripp, I hardly recognize you!"

"I had to come back to thank you again. Your gift has brought me my fortune. It has saved my life and provided me with food and clothing."

"And that is a fortune?" asked Hannah.

"I discovered that all I need is just enough. I desire only two more things."

"What two things?" she asked.

"A soft bed and a mother's love," he replied. He took her hands in his.

"They are yours, gladly." She smiled warmly. "Now I, too, have just enough."

Thoughtful Young

In a Field of Poppies

Avra Margariti

It started when Kate discovered a red-brown spot on her underwear. But that wasn't all, lately, she'd gotten into the habit of binding her chest, so it hadn't grown as much as the other girls' in her grade. It stood to reason she would secretly hope to skip her period altogether. Her lungs felt like they were shrinking with each undulating pulse of pain low in her belly. Breathless, Kate dashed out the front door and toward the poppy fields behind her house.

From the window of the neighboring cottage, Sally spotted her friend sprinting down the dirt path. Sally looked at her doodles in the margins of her English textbook, then at the text itself. The letters swapped places with each other and bled together. This always happened whenever she tried to read a block of text, though she didn't know why. Sally blinked to clear the black-and-white vertigo, then grabbed her messenger bag and chased after Kate.

Oz was checking the air pressure in his bicycle tires when Sally hurried past him and disappeared into the tall grass. Her blond hair was pulled into pigtails, which he enjoyed tugging on when he sat behind her at school, even though he was too old for that now. The determination of her steps piqued Oz's curiosity. With one last glance inside the cottage, where his mother slept beneath a mound of blankets, he hopped onto his bike and followed the track worn down from his many trips over the years.

Kate had screamed herself hoarse, so now she lay exhausted on the poppy-strewn field, glaring up into the sky. Every thought in her mind was a plea for the soil to open up and swallow her traitorous body.

Sally ran up to her. The anger in Kate's scrunched up face and the drops of dried blood on her inner thighs told Sally all she needed to know. Catching her breath, she dug around her bag and retrieved a little white square and a couple of wet wipes.

"Here," she said. "Do you know how to use a pad?"

Kate glanced up at Sally, haloed by the April sun. She cleared her throat. "Thank you."

"The first time I got my period, I thought my body was trying to kill me," Sally said and cracked a smile.

Kate's laughter rang hollow. She knew she wasn't dying, but it still felt that way for reasons she couldn't explain even to herself. With the blood cleaned from her thighs and the pad rubbing uncomfortably against her, she said, "Um, you can turn around now, Sally."

The sound of grass flattened beneath wheels announced Oz's arrival. They watched as he bounced toward them on his rickety bike.

"Great," muttered Kate.

Everyone said Oz's family was a bad lot. At school, Oz was known to bully other kids into trading their lunches with him. Additionally, he didn't grasp the concept of personal space and always had a silly joke or invasive question on the tip of his tongue. Kate only liked Oz when they played soccer in the dirt lot behind school. He said she was better at it than all the boys in their village, and the pride she felt at his words hit her like a sugar rush.

"What do *you* want?" Sally demanded, crossing her arms over her chest. She tried to be brave like Kate, but her voice trembled like a bird's trill.

Oz dismounted and set his bike down among the knee-high grass and bright red poppies. He ran a hand through his crow's-nest hair and grinned. His front tooth was chipped from when he'd crashed his bike into a fence years ago. "I saw you two run into the fields and thought you might be up to something fun."

Kate, still lying on the ground, let out an involuntary groan as a new wave of pain and nausea rolled through her.

"What's wrong with her?"

"Leave her alone, Oswald." Sally glared at him; her eyebrows curled like question marks. Oz's interest was piqued again. He wanted to know what the question was, so he could give her all the answers.

He dropped down next to Kate, unconcerned with the dirt smearing the frayed knees of his cargo pants. "Where does it hurt?"

Although Oz occasionally enjoyed messing with people, nothing was as deep-rooted as his urge to fix things. Fix the ancient bicycle that was all he had left of his dad, fix the leak in his cottage's roof, fix his mother's hangover with coffee and aspirin. So now, as Kate clutched her sides and Sally stood sentry over her, Oz reached into his pocket and, with a magician's flourish, produced a silver packet of pills.

After a moment of hesitation, Kate accepted the aspirin, as well as the grease-stained hand that helped her to her feet. She took a sip from Sally's water bottle and swallowed the pill.

"Better?" Oz asked, softer than before.

Kate scrubbed at the fresh tears pricking the corners of her eyes. "No, not better. This shouldn't have happened." Her voice, which she usually took great care to pitch low and deep, rose high despite herself.

"What do you mean?" Sally asked. Surely Kate knew that getting her period was bound to happen, right?

Kate grabbed fistfuls of her frizzy, wavy hair—much too long for her liking—and tugged in frustration. "That's the thing. I've no idea."

Oz watched her intently. Neither Kate nor Sally had ever seen him this serious.

"Why does anything happen?" he said and kicked up a clump of dirt. "Why did my dad die? Why is my mom still not dealing with it?"

"Why am I so useless at school?" Sally blurted. "Every time I open a book, I think it's going to bite me. Why can't I just make my parents proud?"

All three stared at each other, shock and embarrassment at their impromptu confessions spreading across their faces. Then Oz threw his head back and let out a laugh like a gushing spring. Sally and Kate joined him, their chests swelling with laughter and their eyes damp with too many emotions to name.

After they came down from their laughing fit, the three children lay in the poppy field, their heads bent together and their bodies fanning out like the spokes of Oz's bike.

Kate willed the flowers to shed their petals on her, cover her from head to toe, and let her emerge anew.

Sally inspected the curved petals, turned gossamer by the sun, and the earth-dark, powdery hearts of the poppies. If only she'd brought her sketchbook and watercolors to capture that moment.

Oz gazed up at the flowers, which were considered weeds by some. He thought about gathering a few poppies into a bouquet when Sally and Kate weren't looking. His mother might like a splash of red on their kitchen table when she woke up.

And as each thought their separate poppy thoughts, the soil and grass and stones parted, and the poppies entangled into a net that gently lowered Kate, Sally, and Oz below the rich-smelling earth.

They were surprised, as much as pre-teens can be surprised by magical things.

The heat of the day drained away. Instinctively, they closed their eyes to protect them from the grit and soil. When they opened them again, they were surrounded by the musty coolness of an underground cave network.

"Where are we?" Sally stammered. She gripped Kate's hand, and Kate let her.

Oz wanted to appear tough, but his heart beat an uneven two-step tempo against his chest. He threaded his fingers through Sally's. Connected, they could feel each other's pulse through their wrists, palms, and fingers.

Only Kate felt a calm wash over her—she was a clear, placid lake.

"This way," she found herself saying and pulled along Sally, who in turn pulled Oz.

Their steps echoed off the honeycomb-colored walls and high ceiling. From somewhere up ahead, they heard the steady drip of water. They walked until the claustrophobic tunnels widened to reveal the lake Kate could already feel inside her. Smoky quartz and topaz sprung in jagged clusters along the shoreline. The water was a deep green-blue. It appeared clear, although if the lake had a bottom, it chose not to reveal it.

"What do you think is down there?" asked Sally, her eyes star-strewn and her voice filled with awe.

"Water monsters, maybe?" Oz said, half-hopeful and half-scared.

Kate stood at the edge of the cave floor, the rubber tips of her canvas shoes grazing the lake's still surface. She leaned forward to catch her reflection in the mirror-like aquatic expanse, and her two companions gingerly followed her lead.

Reflected in the water, Kate saw a young man. Tall and sturdy, with a shock of wavy hair cut short above his ears and an easy smile, it looked to Kate like the man knew his place in the world. Something clicked inside her, and more silent tears rolled down her cheeks: this time not of anger, sadness, or confusion, but of validation.

Sally saw a woman. Brushes stuck out of the pockets of her paint-spattered overalls. The flush of her face wasn't due to embarrassment, as Sally's often was, but indicated a warmth and passion emanating from within.

Oz, too, saw a man. He had a stethoscope around his neck, draped over his teddy-bear-print scrubs. He looked a bit neater, with combed hair and a face free of smudges. Still, the wild shine in his eyes remained.

All three reflections were holding hands.

At dusk, they awoke, still lying in their poppy field. They remembered the cave, the lake, and their reflections, and then they didn't. Only the sensation lingered, of things falling into place.

Kate's abdomen hurt again.

Sally winced at the thought of her teacher, and then her parents, finding out she hadn't finished her homework.

Oz worried his mother had woken up from her nap and hadn't found him by her side.

Still, when the three looked at each other, their mouths lifted into identical bright smiles.

"I was thinking," Oz started, scuffing his taped-up sneaker in the dirt, "we could come out to the fields again and hang out. You know. If you wanted."

Sally looked at Oz, with his tousled hair, grass-stained clothes, and shining eyes. "I just decided," she said. "You aren't that bad after all. Tomorrow after school?"

Kate, who wouldn't be called Kate for much longer, nodded eagerly. "Tomorrow sounds good."

Migration

Brian K. Lowe

I first heard about it when Redwood appeared in the desert, dropping his bags with a thud. One of them popped open, spilling a sunrise with scented air redolent with the gradual warming of tree sap and the sound of melting spring snow. Redwood picked it up hurriedly, embarrassed at his own clumsiness. Of course, I didn't know his name was Redwood then—or why. I didn't know why he was there, either—not that I cared. There was room enough for two.

"Hello," I said. "I'm—." It's no good trying to write it. I come from what you might call an oral tradition. It was the sound of dust skittering over rocks. I liked my name.

"Redwood," he said simply.

"Redwood? What kind of name is that?" I wasn't being nosy, just curious. My kind don't get around much. We used to, but with all the people moving in we just sort of stopped.

"I'm from up north," he said as if that explained it all. So I went back to drifting over the rocks, listening to the sound of my own name, and let Redwood do his thing. His "thing" consisted mainly of brooding, but since brooding is a quiet occupation, it sat well with me and the desert.

I ran across Redwood again a few years later, on the western edge of my territory. I'd been feeling a kind of itch there the last few months, and so, saying good-bye to the old tortoise I'd been walking with since autumn, I let myself be blown toward the setting sun. There sat Redwood, brooding harder than ever. He was not alone.

I stopped short, surprised for the first time since the cliff dwellers went away, all in one night.

"Well, hello!" I said to the one whose name was the sound of a fish breaking the surface of the lake to the west. I spoke her name with pleasure, for long ago she and I had shared some of the same territory. Her smile was subdued and sad.

"Hello—," she said to me, stumbling a bit over my name. "You may call me Waterlily now."

"'Waterlily'?" I repeated. This name business was getting to be too much for me. Too many changes. "What kind of name is that?" This time I was not being curious, I was being nosy.

"It's what the people call one of the flowers that used to grow on my lake," she explained.

"People? On your lake?" I was frowning now. "Since when?"

"For years now. It started with only a few, but now they are everywhere. Houses, cars, people... They ran so many boats over my lake that they frightened the fish away—those they didn't eat. So they brought in new fish to hunt, and they multiplied too fast and poisoned the water and ate all of the plants. The more people there were, the less room there was for me. And finally I stopped being (the sound of a fish breaking the surface of the lake) and just became Waterlily."

She stared out over my empty, open desert. It almost seemed to stretch into infinity; the dry winds swept across my lands without boundaries until they met the snow-capped mountains far, far away. I felt the winds; it was a good feeling, and I reveled in it, but I knew that I could never share it with her. Each of us had chosen his land long ago, as it pleased us, and none could change now. Though I knew it to be useless, I offered my old friend the range of my home, even as I had Redwood.

"There is room for all," I told her, but she only looked at me with sadness and pity, and I didn't know why.

She thanked me. "I will accept your hospitality for as long as you can offer it, but soon you will be as homeless as we are."

I shook my head. "No. People will not want it. The desert is too vast, too dry. Since the cave dwellers left, almost no one comes here, and no one ever stays."

Redwood glanced up from his brooding for the first time, perhaps for the first time since we had last met.

"She's right. The same happened to me. I roamed a million acres of forest when I was younger, but people came and chopped it down for their cities, piece by piece, acre by acre. It is only a shadow of what it once was. What people do not destroy, they engulf. One night I went to sleep as (the color of every pine needle on every tree at once) and when I awoke the next day, I was what they had made me: I was Redwood. Since then I have wandered from space to space, and every time people have come upon the wild places and covered them with houses and roads and cities. They will cover over this place, too, and the name of (dust skittering over rocks) will be gone, and only sand will remain."

I shook my head and would not hear of it. I retreated to the cliffs where men had once lived, but no more. Of all my lands, this was where people most often came now, but alone or in small numbers, and always taking great care not to change the placement of a single stone. As long as they left me alone, I did the same for them.

I found people there now. They disturbed nothing; they only looked and drew pictures. But still upset at what Waterlily and Redwood had said, I blew up a dust storm and watched with malicious glee as they ran for their vehicle and roared away.

I had never seen people leave in such a hurry before. I had never realized how their cars scarred the sandstone and how badly they smelled.

Years passed, as time is measured by people. I had been avoiding the western edge of my territory, telling myself that I wanted to leave it to Waterlily and Redwood, so that they might find the peace and solitude they had lost along with their homes. But I was lying to myself. The itching I had felt was not going away.

The animals knew, of course. They were steadily migrating eastward; their habitat being eaten by creeping degrees. Some stayed, the snakes and the birds, and the insects, who can survive almost anything. But other than the insects, those who stayed either died or followed their fellows into exile. Often they did both.

The first machines felt like the biting of insects on my arm. It was an odd sensation: I've never been bitten by an insect. But there it was, and I couldn't avoid it any longer. People had come into my territory, come to stay, and unlike the cliff dwellers, they didn't take my land the way they found it. They took it and made of it what they would.

I found Redwood and Waterlily packing their bags— memories, smells, colors laid just so. In the years of his guesting with me, Redwood had obviously come to appreciate my land: Palettes of desert sunset lay beside the dappled greens of his homeland.

Waterlily had never liked the desert, but I knew that of old; she was a water spirit; she loved her lakes and her reeds and water plants and croaking frogs and slippery fishes. Still, she was plainly sad to go.

I stood there staring at them both, my eyes blazing so mad the winds were whipping up dust devils. If those builder people could have seen the spot where I was standing right now, I believe they would have turned tail and run.

"Well, where are you two going?" I demanded. When I get roused, wind blows and dust flies in clouds and the air crackles with my anger, but Redwood and Waterlily used to do the same kind of thing, back when they had homes, so they weren't at all impressed.

"We're leaving," Redwood said. "Maybe we can go live in the mountains for a while. I might find some trees, and Waterlily might even find another lake." Waterlily nodded mournfully, and the heartbreak I saw in her, she who had once been mine, made me even more furious. That I could never give her what she wanted made me madder still.

"We can fight them, damn it!" I cried, unaware that I was already showing the signs, that I was already using human terms that should have held no meaning for me at all. "You are (sound of a fish breaking the surface of the lake) and (color of all the pine needles in the forest at once), and I am (dust skittering over the rocks)! We have roamed these lands for thousands of years, us and the animal spirits and the water babies and..." I stopped, because I could see their thoughts, and I knew they were right even if I wouldn't admit it.

All the animal spirits and the water babies and the others were gone, chased away by people cutting down their forests and covering their caves and burrows with houses and roads and sidewalks. We were the last, the spirits of the land, and we were only hanging on by our fingernails. They used to worship us, called us elementals and guardians of the land and the trees and the water; now they just ignored us and raped the land and dammed up the streams to satisfy their lusts for money and to find "unspoiled" places to live. But no sooner did they someplace "simpler" than they wanted all the same roads and stores and conveniences that made their old homes "too crowded," so they moved again, not caring that they were crowding out the plants and animals—and us.

Redwood and Waterlily left quietly in the night, while I was watching the people scrape away at the edges of my land. I saw one run his truck over a 75-year-old tortoise and never stop. The wind howled—I howled—but they just rolled up the windows on their trucks to keep the dust out. They worked all night under their big lights because it was so hot during the day. I fought them with everything I had: Not a day went by that the men didn't curse the sand in the gears of their machinery or the constant storms that blinded them.

"I am (dust skittering over rocks)!" I shouted in their deaf ears. A few of them wondered to themselves if they had accidentally disturbed some cursed Indian burial ground, but they never came near the truth, no matter how many beers they poured down their dust-coated throats.

But they never quit, either. They built houses that could keep out the dust, and planted trees to cut down the wind. I spent months fighting with every weapon I owned, and it didn't do any good. To the east my desert was bordered by mountains, in the west by the houses of men.

More came, with more machines, and still I fought. At least I could slow them down, I thought. Some of the animals can still escape. And some did, but the plants were not so lucky. The spines of the thorniest cactus were useless against men in steel machines. They died, uprooted, and the birds and insects who lived in them fled or died.

They laid down roads, filing the skin from my land, pushing always eastward toward the mountains where Redwood and Waterlily had gone. The fingers of "civilization" pressed me hard as I fought.

"I am (dust skittering over rocks)!" I cried, but they paid no attention.

One day men drove to the very center of my territory, cars and trucks and vehicles in a long thin line, raising a dust cloud that lay brown on the blue sky for miles. There were pipes and bulldozers on those trucks, and they brought cement mixers and rollers and machines whose names I had yet to learn, but I hated all the same.

They put up metal huts in the center of my land and they drove stakes into the ground and made measurements and drew maps and began to roll and rumble over all the land and plants and animals that formed the heart of me. And on the westward side, on the side of the road they had made that lead back to their city, they put up a sign: Coming soon. A new city of tomorrow, bright and clean as the desert sun. *A new city of tomorrow, built on the forgotten bones of yesterday.*

I flew into my greatest rage. I cried: "I am (dust skittering over rocks)!" as the men huddled in their tin shelters and awaited the abatement of my storm. "I am (dust skittering over rocks)!" I screamed as I raked their bulldozers with wind-blown sand so fiercely that the paint was scoured from the metal. "I am (dust skittering over rocks)!" I shouted as I plucked their impertinent, childishly self-important sign from the ground and flung it through the air and buried it with dirt.

"That is the power of (dust skittering over rocks)," I said to them triumphantly as they stumbled out of their metal houses into the next morning's bright, hot sunshine. But they did not hear me. They marveled and shook their heads at the carnage I had wrought, but then they cleaned their bulldozers and their trucks and went back to work. They found their sign and pounded it back into place. They scraped and leveled and graded and poured and hammered and built. They covered my heart with cement.

At long last I packed my bags. I made the long journey to the mountains in the tracks of Redwood and Waterlily. When I arrived, I met a mountain spirit who lived there.

"Welcome," he said. "I am (cold of midwinter snow)."

"Hello," I said to him. "My name is Sand."

The Prince and the Giant

Alphayo O Oduor

There once lived a king who had a son, Prince Zawadi, who was very stubborn, he was also arrogant and foolish, always reminding those around him that he was the prince. The servants in the palace did not like him

But despite all these behaviours, He was the king's favourite as he was the only surviving heir to the throne after his father.

King Chacha always tried to talk to his son to change his behavior, but the prince never took heed to his father's advice. The king was always worried as he knew if his son doesn't change then he may end up leading Baraka kingdom badly, hence being a bad king, soiling all the good deeds his father worked for during his reign. Deeds done for the betterment of the Kingdom of Baraka.

Chacha became a worried man but despite that, he had hopes that one day Prince Zawadi would change his bad behaviours.

Time went by but there was no indication of him changing, this got the king to be more worried than ever.

In the center of Baraka kingdom there was a very big forest which the people knew to be inhabited by giants. They called it the evil forest. Long ago a wall was built, with but a single gate was put in place to prevent people from going to the forest and the giants from coming to the kingdom.

No living Barakan had ever gone past the gate, except one person. This person, who was believed to have gone to the evil forest was Mumu, the kingdom's witch doctor.

It is believed that Mumu fought with the giants and defeated them because he had powers of witchcraft.

One chilly morning when the birds were still singing their melodious songs thanking God for another day, Prince

71

Zawadi came early to the king's room. This surprised King Chacha. It was not common for his son to be up so early in the day.

"Son?" he asked. "I hope all is well. Why are you up this early?"

"I am going for a walk."

This, the king knew, was unusual. "And where would you walk?" asked the king.

I am going through the gate and into the evil forest.

At this the king, who was still in bed, sat up in his bed and looked directly at his son thinking his son had run mad.

"That is foolish," insisted the king. But his son insisted, not only was he foolish but he was stubborn.

"Son why are you always stubborn?" the king asked Zawadi. But the Prince insisted and all the king's words turned on deaf ears.

And leaving his father sitting on his bed, Prince Zawadi set off his journey to the evil forest.

It was not long before he reached the main entrance to the gate, which was always manned by the kingdom guards. He ordered the gate to be opened which the guards had no choice but to do, for it was as the prince had ordered. And alone and filled with pride, the prince set forth on the journey inside the evil forest.

Not far inside the evil forest there lived a giant, known to his people as Bobo, who owned a beautiful garden which had many different trees which had different fruits that were always ripe. This giant had built himself a large castle and lead his fellow giants, who had much respect for him, as their king.

Unused to walking, Zawadi grew very tired and thirsty. Finding Bobo's grove, he ate of Bobo's fruits and lay down and took a nap under a tree.

It was usual for Bobo the Giant King to go round the forest to monitor his kingdom. This morning brought him to the very tree where the Prince slept.

"Who is this in my kingdom?" the giant asked angrily when he saw Prince Zawadi sleeping under the tree, the husks and cores of his fruits scattered about.

Zawadi was awakened by the thunderous voice. He began to shiver with fear when he saw the giant. Bobo the giant was as tall as a pineous tree, his roar was as thunder.

Bobo reached down and grasped Zawadi and lifted him up if to swallow him, his mouth wide and big enough to eat a cow.

"Please, master giant, do not eat me. I am a prince and this is my father's kingdom.

Birds throughout the forest took to wing at the giant's laugh. "You are the prince?" said the giant." That's nonsense, but I shall eat you anyway."

Prince Zawadi begged the giant to let him go, swearing never to return to the forest again. But it was in vain, Prince Zawadi's arrogant and foolish life ended as Bobo the giant swallowed him and he was no more.

Back home the king knew he would never see his son again, his foolishness and arrogance had been the end of him, for no one who goes to the evil forest comes back again.

Thoughtful Young

Six Legs, Three Heads

Jenny Blackford

The alien had six legs, three heads, and long, gray-blue fur, almost the same color as my oldest pair of blue jeans, the ones Mum always wants to throw out. Lexie and I just stared at it for a few minutes after it appeared. Was it real, or had we been playing handball too long in the afternoon sun? School was over, but the playground was still hot as a barbecue grill.

There were kids kicking balls and yelling over on the sports field, and teachers were around somewhere, but Lexie and I had been playing handball against the old brick wall for so long that everyone had lost interest. We were the only ones close enough to see the alien–if it *was* real.

Then it started to talk to us.

"Take me to your uncle," it said, and waggled some of its twelve ears—or the things that looked like ears, stuck here and there all around its heads. It had four ear-thingies on each head, which made it look fairly odd, with its six legs and blue-jeans fur and everything. There were tentacles as well, but every time I tried to count them, I got to about five, then some of them moved, and I lost track.

Lexie and I stared at the alien for another minute, while we walked a bit closer. Lexie looked pretty silly, I thought, with her mouth wide open, despite those big green eyes and that long brown hair. Then I realized that my own mouth was open and closed it.

That helped me to think of the next thing to do. I said, "What?"

I'm always quick under stress.

"Sorry, I forgot," it said. "Take me to your uncle, *please.*"

The alien's tentacles shimmered in and out of view. It seemed to be waiting for one of us to say something.

I couldn't imagine anyone wanting to talk to my Uncle Nick, especially after what had happened with Dad's ride-on lawnmower last year; but Lexie has so many uncles that one of them might be interesting enough for an alien to visit.

"Uncle Braydon or Uncle Jayden or Uncle Jarrod or—" Lexie said, but then, luckily, the alien interrupted her.

"Sorry, 'uncle' was the wrong word."

"Did you mean 'aunt'?" asked Lexie. I could easily imagine an alien wanting to meet her Auntie Madison. She's seriously interesting. Not many aunties teach karate and write video games.

"Actually, no, not 'aunt' either. It's tricky..." The alien suddenly held, in one of its tentacles, something like a purple banana with lots of silver knobs. It pointed the purple banana at us and pressed one of the buttons.

For a moment, I froze in fear. I tried to stand in front of Lexie, but she pushed me aside so she was standing next to me again.

The alien put the banana-shaped weapon up to one of its heads, spoke into it, and seemed to listen for an answer. It lowered the weapon and said, "Take me to your *leader*, please."

Oh. The weapon was a translator.

But what should we tell the alien?

Lexie looked at me, and I looked back at her. Her big, green eyes were very wide. "*Leader*," she mouthed at me silently, with a meaningful look. I knew what she meant. When this happens on TV, it means the aliens are going to invade the Earth.

Before I could think of anything sensible to say, she turned to the alien and said, "Why? And who are you?"

"My name is Zorkblap-bleep," (or, at least, that is what it sounded like to us.) "I am a representative of the ancient and powerful race of Krelnnn. We have come to conquer your puny little planet."

Oh-oh. The aliens really *were* here to invade Earth.

The alien was still talking away. "We have a huge invasion force stationed on the next planet out," it said. "I believe you call it *Mars*. Resistance is futile."

I took a deep breath. "Why are *you* here, if the rest of your people are on Mars?" I said. "And why have you come to our schoolyard?"

It's weird, but neither of us was really scared. Maybe it was just the cuddly blue-jeans-colored fur. We *should* have been scared, of course. Any alien who's been beamed down onto Earth must have some pretty special technology backing it up.

"Schoolyard?" Zorkblap-bleep replied. "A place for young Earthlings to play during the years when they are being educated in a communal manner?"

I thought for a minute. "Yes, that's what this is," I said, and pointed all around at the basketball hoops and the monkey bars and everything.

The alien's furry ears waggled madly. "You mean this is not your Global Government? I am not in the right place?"

"Um, no." Obviously.

I tried to think, fast. An alien was looking for our Global Government as a start to conquering the Earth. I breathed deeply for a moment, then I gave the alien a quick run-down on the difference between an inner-Sydney Aussie Primary School and a Global Government–including the fact that there is no Global Government on Earth, yet. Or maybe ever, the way the politicians are going.

"So," I finished up, "why do you want to conquer the Earth anyway?"

Its ears wriggled, presumably expressing some mysterious alien emotion or other. "Actually, I'm not sure. I'm the exotic language expert, not one of the military. I wanted them to send someone else down with me, but they were all busy on Mars."

I said, "You don't know *why* you're trying to conquer Earth?"

"No," it replied. "The climate on Mars is so much better. A resort there would be delightful! Those cool low-oxygen breezes in the twilight—so relaxing. The dust is so good for the fur. And such a lovely view of Saturn and Jupiter by night."

I had no idea what to say to that. Luckily, the alien language expert just loved to talk.

"Do you think that conquering Earth is a bad idea, then?"

Lexie and I looked at one another. Yes, it was definitely a bad idea, but how were we going to convince him?

She stood up very straight. She said to it, "If you're the exotic languages expert, I guess you think we're pretty exotic."

"Oh, yes," it said, "you humans are fabulously rare and fascinating. Bipeds! Amazing! How do you balance, with only two legs? We watch nature documentaries about you for hours. And we just love your films and TV, especially the science fiction."

If this had been a cartoon, a little light bulb would have come on over Lexie's head. She winked at me, then made her face go all serious as she turned back to the alien.

She said, "If you've seen a lot of our science fiction movies, you should have some idea what we exotic bipeds would think about blue alien overlords."

"Oh," it said worriedly, if you can imagine a blue alien sounding worried. "Like *Mars Attacks*."

In a firm tone, Lexie said, "We would rather destroy the whole planet than submit. And we would keep on fighting forever, until we found some way to win. Zorkblap-bleep, do you remember *Independence Day*?"

It nodded two of its heads. The other one looked undecided.

Lexie clearly has a great future ahead of her as a diplomat one day. "Even if you win, the Earth will be a total mess. No one will be able to make any new movies or TV shows. There won't be any more Terminator movies. Or Star Trek."

"No more Star Trek?" Zorkblap said, waggling its ears madly. "That's terrible! I give in. But how can I convince the soldiers? They're determined to conquer this planet."

Lexie put on her best serious look—the one she uses when she asks hard questions in class. "My Auntie Madison swore me to secrecy, but maybe it would be in the best interests of Earth if I tell you about the Anti-Matter Planet Destructor she designed."

Wow! Lexie's aunt was even more interesting than I'd thought!

"Please tell me, young Earthling," Zorkblap-bleep replied. "I must stop the Krelnnn from destroying the Earth! Life on Krelnnnar would not be worth living without Earthling science fiction! Please give me a reason that I can explain to them."

"Deep inside the deepest mountain," Lexie said, "there's a secret cave of ice, invisible to radar or any other form of scientific detection. Only Auntie Madison knows where it is. Inside it, miraculously suspended from the icy roof, there are two giant gems as big as elephants: a huge red ruby, and a green anti-ruby just as huge. They're this far apart."

She held her two hands out, so close that I could barely see sunlight between them.

"If they ever touch, the whole Earth will explode, and the blast will be so huge that it will destroy Mars as well."

She pointed at Zorkblap-bleep. "The only thing that keeps the ruby and the anti-ruby apart, and stops the Earth being blown to tiny pieces, is the force of my Aunt Madison's mind. She concentrates on them all day and all night, even when she's asleep. And she's not afraid to use it! If she stops for even a moment..." She shuddered theatrically. "Boom!"

Zorkblap-bleep was shivering in fear. I have to admit, I was worried too. What if Lexie's Auntie Madison got distracted one day?

Zorkblap-bleep said, "I will return to the mothership and explain everything to my leaders. We will not try to conquer Earth. You have proven it is just not worth it."

Lexie and I agreed vigorously.

"And I will keep your secret," it said. "I am honored that you trusted me with it."

Lexie blushed and nodded.

Zorkblap-bleep walked back a few steps, waggled the purple banana at us cheerfully, and blinked out of sight.

"Phew," I said to Lexie. "Well done. You were amazing."

"It was nothing," she said, but she went pink. I think she was pleased.

I couldn't help asking. I had to know. "Is it true? About the ruby and the anti-ruby?"

"Kind of," Lexie said, looking a bit embarrassed. "It was in a video game that Auntie Madison designed." She giggled, then I started to laugh, and couldn't stop. Soon, she was laughing like a mad thing too, with tears running down her cheeks. Every time I managed to stop, she said, "Video game," and I started laughing again. When she stopped, I said, "Anti-Matter Planet Destructor," and that started her off again.

When we finally both ran out of laughter and I caught my breath, I said, "There's no point telling our parents about this, is there?"

"No," she said, panting slightly. "Or anybody else, for that matter."

That was a relief. Nobody would ever have believed us.

So we went back to the still-warm brick wall, chuckling now and then, and played handball for a while, as if it was a perfectly ordinary afternoon after school.

That was three months ago, and we've never talked about how we saved the Earth from destruction by an ancient and powerful race of aliens. But just occasionally, Lexie catches my eye and holds her hands close together, like the giant ruby and the anti-ruby almost touching one another, and we both double over, helplessly laughing and laughing.

The Fox Child

Parker Yancey

In a far-away valley, there lived a fox child. She lived alone in the forest, under the roots of a large tree. Every morning, she went out, careful as she could, watching the sky warily. She went about her day, always under her friends, the trees, who protected her. She visited the hard-working beavers by the river, or the wise deer by their lake, and even the funny frogs that made her laugh with their jokes. But she would never leave the shelter of the trees.

Every night, before she went to sleep, she climbed the tallest tree on the edge of her forest and sat on the second-highest branch. From there she would look up at the cliff.

For there was a tree, at the top of that cliff, that held peaches. Wonderful, fuzzy, and golden. The fox child had never eaten one for peaches did not grow under tall trees—but she dreamed of the day when she could. Nothing was in her way; she could scamper up those cliffs easier than she could climb the trees. But she was scared.

The fox child wasn't scared of the cunning black ravens of the cliffs—she was big enough to whack them—and she wasn't scared of the large, gray wolves, who were like brothers to her. She wasn't even scared of the great, red dragon, whom she thought had easier things to catch.

No, she wasn't scared of any of them.

The fox child was scared of the sky.

It was so *large*, and so *high*, and yet it seemed like it would reach down and swallow her up in bigness if she dared step out of the trees. She had never seen the sky at night. The very thought terrified her. So, every night, she went to sleep saddened, because the peaches were out of her reach.

One day, the fox child sat on the second-highest branch and looked at the peaches much earlier than usual. She was bored. The beavers were visiting their family upriver, the deer were nowhere to be found, and the frogs had made fun of her large ears. They did that a lot, but today? Today she was sadder than usual. The peaches just sat there, like they did every year around this time, with nobody to eat them. The cliff was too tall for the wolves, and the raven didn't like peaches, apparently. And the dragon, well, he was a dragon.

She sighed. She could climb those smaller cliffs. Her hands and feet were sure, she could climb the tallest trees in the forest faster than anyone! And then she could eat the peaches. But... the sky was *clear* today. She shivered, and shook her head. No. Not today. One day, though. Maybe when there were more clouds.

She was so bored and unhappy, she barely cared when the great red dragon swooped down to land next to her tree.

"Why are you so sad, fox child?" he rumbled.

"I want to eat the peaches," she cried in desperation. "I always see them, but I can never eat them."

The dragon looked up the cliffs to the old peach tree. "Why do you not eat them, small one?"

She shied back against the trunk of the tree. "The sky is there," she whispered. "It will swallow me."

The dragon gave a great laugh that shook the leaves. "Small one, I am a dragon. I can swallow you. But the sky is an old friend of mine, he does not eat little fox children like you." The wise, red dragon looked back at her, and then saw her wide eyes. She did not fear him, who could snap her up without a second thought. But she truly feared his old friend sky, whom he flew with every day. The dragon was old, but he had never, in all his days under the sky, seen anything like this. "Small one...how will you ever get a peach?"

"Wait until the sky leaves? It's been waiting there for *years*, it has to leave one of these days." she replied, voice filled with hope, clambering to the edge of the branch, where she looked longingly at the fruit-laden tree. He moved his massive head closer, and she jumped back into the shadows of the second-highest branch.

"What if I helped you. Covered you with my wings, so that the sky could not see you. Would you go to the tree then?"

The fox child peered from the shadows. "But you are a dragon, you would eat me."

"Not when I am curious."

She looked at the peaches imploringly, then at the dragon. "Why do you want to help me? Do you want a peach, too?"

"Little one, I could eat all the peaches in the world. I do not need a peach. Will you come with me?" Hesitantly, she slid to the ground. The dragon was big, and he could eat her. But he was not as big as the sky. She looked to the cliff where the fuzzy peaches waved in the wind. The dragon spread a great wing, and darkness fell over her. She gasped as the sky disappeared. It couldn't see her!

The fox child ran, fast as she could, and the shadow of the dragon followed her all the way to the cliff. She had never felt grass so soft—maybe it wasn't scared of the sky like she was—and she laughed as she ran.

They reached the rocky cliff. The fox child looked to the dragon and began to climb. His great shadow covered her, and the rocks fell beneath her feet quickly. "See, small one, the sky cannot reach you under my wing."

"Thank you, great dragon!" she said happily. She was going to make it! She would eat the peaches and—

The shadow disappeared. The sun shone on her as the dragon winged into...the sky. She froze, the breeze and the sunlight brushing over her. The deep of the sky rose above her, pulling her eyes heavenward. It looked down at her, great and vast and.... She cried out in fear and scrambled up the cliff, rising higher and higher until grass once more was beneath her. There was a tree. She bolted under it, hiding her face from the impossible bigness of the sky.

The sun warmed her head and rustled her hair. Nothing happened. She wasn't sucked up, forever and ever, to be eaten by the blueness. Then something fell on her head. She yelped in surprise, almost poking her head out. But it wasn't a rock...or a clod of dirt... It was soft.

Opening her eyes, the child peeked under her arm. There, rolling slowly towards the edge, was a peach. She scrambled towards it, reaching for the small golden fruit—and it fell. She shouted and threw herself forward to catch it and found herself falling. Something soft fell into her hands, and she clutched it close as she tumbled down the cliff.

Rocks bashed at her, bruising and cracking all over her. Tears came to her eyes as the sky and the earth spun around her. She came to rest at the bottom, on the soft grass, facing the sky. Her breath caught, and she just lay, looking up into the dark bigness of the great sky.

It didn't reach down to swallow her.

The fox child sat up, hurt twinging through her. And she realized there was something in her hand, the thing she had protected in the fall. And then her eyes widened and the hurt went away as she saw that in her hand, sat a perfect, golden peach.

Snow

James Dorr

"Hi there," the platinum blonde in the ball gown said. "My name's Snow. It's short for Snow White. They call me that because my hair's so white, it's almost snow-colored, even though I'll only be sixteen on my next birthday. And you must be"— she paused and counted on her fingers, using both hands— "seven dwarves!"

"We prefer to be called 'little people," the chief dwa—little person said. "These are Squinty, Snoozy, Smelly, Sappy, Slappy, and Whatsit, and my name's Seymour. They call us that because Squinty here's—"

"I'm sure that must be fascinating," Snow cut him off, "but don't you want to know what a girl like me's doing out here in the middle of the Forbidden Forest, in only my ball gown?"

"Not particularly," Seymour said. "We're on our way home from a hard day's work at the mine." He gestured toward the heavy, lumpy sacks all seven carried slung on their backs. "We really don't have time for idle chit-chat. Have a nice day."

Snow stamped her foot. "That's not very nice! I'm here in the woods because my evil stepmother, Evelyn—she's queen of the land on the other side of the Stagnant Lake, by the way—told her huntsman, Humbert, to drag me into the forest's center and cut out my heart. But Humbert thought that would be too messy, so he just left me here instead, to die of whatever it is people die of when they're left in the middle of the forest."

"Well, have a good time then," Seymour said, "but it's getting late. Let us know if you ever find out what it is you'll die of."

"Wait a minute!" Snow shouted. "You're not supposed to just leave me here. You're supposed to rescue me!"

"With a temper like yours?" Seymour started to say, but just then Sappy whispered in his ear. Then Whatsit whispered something in his other ear too. The three conversed further, with the other little people joining in as well.

Finally, Seymour turned back to Snow. "Can you cook?" he asked.

Snow thought for a moment—one didn't really learn how to cook when one's raised in a palace, but there couldn't be all that much to it. Put something in a pot. Pour in some water. Pop it, pot and all, into the fireplace. Pull it out when it starts to smell too bad. And she *did* need to be rescued.

"Uh, yeah?" she said.

The little people conversed among themselves some more.

"And I also can make beds and do light housework."

"Deal," Seymour said.

oOo

Back in the palace, the evil queen, Evelyn, had just received Humbert the huntsman's report. "Just like you predicted, your majesty, she opted for being abandoned in the forest when I offered her the choices."

"She's a good girl," Queen Evelyn muttered, dismissing the huntsman. "Maybe a little too good at times, though. But let me see what the mirror has to say."

She went to her bedroom, admiring her neatly made-up bed. Something she'd have to do for herself now, she thought. At least for a while—that was the downside. She prowled to her dressing table and sat in its comfortable chair, facing the mirror.

"Magic Mirror next to the wall, has Snow thus far survived it all?"

"She has, my queen, and don't be snitty, but so you know, she's getting pretty."

"Well, yes, that too," Evelyn muttered. While the mirror didn't dare to say it, she herself wasn't getting any younger.

She rose from her chair, then strode to the pantry where the kitchen staff kept the apples.

oOo

"What do you guys mine?" Snow asked that night, after she'd fixed them a nutritious supper of boiled dead rabbit. She'd found the rabbit out by the highway, but scuffed it up so the hoof prints didn't show.

"Jewels," Smelly said, pointing to the big safe that Seymour had just locked.

"Emeralds and rubies and diamonds," Squinty added. "Diamonds, especially, are going up on the market right now. A few more hauls like we got today, and I bet we could put in for early retirement."

"Fascinating," Snow said.

"Indeed," Slappy said. "Tonight, while the rest of us are asleep, Snoozy will put them all in their settings, with silver and gold chains and rings and all kinds of things that'll make 'em worth even more. Snoozy likes to do this because he's an insomniac—kind of ironic, don't you think, considering his name?"

"I'm sure," Snow said. She was kind of tired too. When bedtime came, she took Snoozy's bed and with the others, Snoozy excepted, was soon fast asleep.

The following day when the little people went back to their mine, she made the beds, then puttered about the hovel doing light housework. Along about lunchtime though, she was interrupted by an old woman—who oddly looked a lot like Queen Evelyn except, of course, old—with a basket of apples. "Buy of my apples, dearie," the old woman cackled. "They're good for your health."

"Well, I don't have any money," Snow said. "The dwa—er, little people and I haven't discussed an allowance yet. Did you know, by the way, that you look a lot like my evil stepmother, Queen Evelyn? That is, like she'd look if she was a lot older."

"Dumb as a rock," the old woman muttered. "But she'll learn. She'll learn." She reached into her basket. "I bet they call you Snow," she said, "because your hair is such a pretty snow white. So I'll tell you what, I'll give you the first apple free as a sample. Just go over there by the couch to eat it, so you'll have something soft to fall into if, for some reason, you should have to fall down. Just be sure to put the half-eaten apple next to you when you do."

Snow did as she was instructed. She moved to the couch, bit into the apple, croaked "Poison!" once, then fell onto the couch being careful, first, to be sure the apple fell onto the cushion next to her head.

oOo

The little people were devastated when they returned from their day at the mine, with seven new sacks stuffed full with jewels. But other than Slappy cuffing Sappy when the latter asked if that meant they could eat Snow, the seven little people went about their routine as usual, because that was all they knew how to do. They ate a cold supper of roots and berries and flies' eggs and mushrooms and then all went to bed, except for Snoozy who opened the safe and toiled through the night, crafting the jewels into earrings and bracelets and pendants and lavaliers, locking them up again, finally, when the first rays of dawn shone through the window.

The next day they went to work, then did the same things that night as before. They thought they might bury Snow eventually, once she began to smell, but for now she looked so lifelike and pretty—almost as pretty as Queen Evelyn, Squinty opined, who once had visited the kingdom across the Stagnant Lake on his vacation.

"Indeed, in a few years when Queen Evelyn gets old, Snow might have become even prettier," Seymour said. He'd once paid a visit there himself. "Too bad the queen's so evil, although I suppose no one can have it all."

Then the next day they went back to work, and on and on till the following Thursday. By now the safe had become so full it could scarcely hold anything more.

oOo

"Magic Mirror, don't give me hype," Queen Evelyn intoned. "Do you think Snow and company are ripe?"

"Don't sneak in like that, all quiet and lurky. Yes, I think it's time to pluck this turkey."

The queen put on her old woman costume again, just in case someone saw her as she crossed into the Forbidden Forest, Humbert having rowed her across the Stagnant Lake, then unpacked a cart from the boat as well to drag behind them. Soon they arrived at the little people's hovel, which the queen entered without even knocking on the door.

"Hsst, Snow," she whispered, waving enchanted smelling salts under the younger woman's nose. "Time to be up and about for your lessons."

"My," Snow said, stretching. "Have I been asleep?"

The queen nodded. "Now watch carefully," she said as she slinked to the safe. "This is a standard combination lock, so what you need to do is listen for the little clicks—yes, like that one! Then, in the other direction—another! And now the third."

She opened the safe's door and Humbert began to load the cart. "You see," Evelyn said, "if you're to grow up to be an evil queen like me, it's not enough to just order your subjects around. After all, someone could break into *your* safe. So there are some things you must learn to be able to do for yourself."

"I think I understand," Snow said. She helped Humbert load the last of the jewelry onto the cart, then watched as Evelyn closed the safe door and gave the lock a final twirl.

"This way," Evelyn said, "they might not even look in the safe, they'll be so surprised that your body is gone. They'll probably spend the whole night looking for you. After all, they saw the apple next to your head, and could tell it was poisoned—it wouldn't be like you'd just stepped out to go to the outhouse."

"Speaking of that, Stepmom."

Evelyn nodded. "Hurry up, though, Snow."

The evil queen smiled. The kid had learned at least that much, to go before you started the trip. Then later, on the boat as Humbert was rowing them back across the lake, Snow looked up at Evelyn, sitting in the stern trying on some of the nicer tiaras.

"Stepmom," she said, "I still don't understand something. Why did I have to eat the poisoned apple at all? That is, I know all it did was make me sleep, but since the dwa—the little guys were going to be away in the daytime anyway, why even go to that much trouble? Besides, what if they *had* buried me?"

"So many questions. But you're learning child. As for being accidentally buried. Had anything happened the mirror would have known. But for the whole thing, it gives you an alibi. The little people won't suspect you, because they think you're dead, and they also know there's a medical school three kingdoms over, on the other side of the forest."

"You mean?"

"Yes, Snow," Evelyn said. "They'll naturally assume that it was grave robbers who saw your body, and copped it to sell the docs so they could use it for dissection class. And as for the jewels—well, even grave robbers don't get that much pay..."

Evelyn saw her stepdaughter's face brighten. Even if maybe a trifle slow, the kid had potential. Evil queens had a way of knowing things like that—even without asking their magic mirrors. And as for her, soon enough it would be time to take the lion's share of the loot and retire to, oh, someplace nice, like Bermuda. Some place warm and sunny while one still had the figure to wear a bikini.

"Also," she said, "when you become queen, it's important to keep your subjects' welfare always in mind—especially the rich ones. To keep them happy. And one way to do that is with outside income that helps you keep their taxes low."

Moral: When it comes to evil queens, the step-apple rarely falls far from the tree.

A Rare and Monstrous Flower

Michelle F. Goddard

Jaxina glanced around the presentation hall and tried to keep her tail from swishing back and forth. The space was full of works of heart-stirring art, ingenious and practical inventions and clever discoveries with promising applications, all for the most important ceremony of their young lives: The Offering of Worthiness.

In front of her sat her presentation; her dying and wilting presentation. Jaxina reached down and ran her fingers over the pale fronds of her anemone, compelling the plant to grow as her mother, Ciminy had shown her. Her mother's fingers had danced and her plants had bloomed, their flexible fronds bending and waving gracefully in the current. Ciminy had made it seem so easy.

Jaxina remembered how intently she had studied those gestures, copying her mother's elegant flourishes; certain she need only follow the pattern perfectly to find success.

"How?" Jaxina had begged of her mother, when perfection became elusive. "There must be some secret technique."

Ciminy would only shake her head and say, "you must find your own way."

Jaxina flicked her tail in irritation. Why would she need to find her own way, when her mother's way was obviously the right way. But now here in the presentation hall, no matter what she did, the plant before her refused to comply. It barely moved in the water currents except when a single tiny branch broke and floated away.

"Pathetic," said a voice from behind her. "Why are you wasting your time with that?" Lorbeth swam forward, brushing her chartreuse tresses from off her shoulder. "It isn't even that special."

"And where is your offering?" Jaxina asked.

"Haven't gotten it yet." Lorbeth grinned as she wrapped her fins around Jaxina's in their secret-sharing grip. "But I know exactly where it is."

"Where, what is?"

"The Umbra Orchid."

Jaxina flinched at the name, her fins flaring in surprise and shock. "That is a myth. It doesn't even exist."

"That's what you know."

"I know," Jaxina said, "trying to find it is a lost cause." Bending low, she crooned and blew bubbles. With fluttering fingers, she funneled them toward her plant. The remaining fronds waved merrily for a moment but then sagged in apathy.

Lorbeth snorted a laugh. "Maybe, if you stop being difficult, I'll let you come with me."

With a flick of her long green tail, Lorbeth swam away. Two more stalks from Jaxina's plant broke off. Caught in the wave of Lorbeth's departure, they flew out among the school of mer-teens. Jaxina stared at her plant as the rest of the branches withered. Her friend was right about something, Jaxina's offering was pathetic.

"Wait, Lorbeth. Wait for me."

Lorbeth spared a grin over her shoulder before speeding away. Jaxina, always the stronger swimmer, easily closed the gap. "Where are we going?"

Lorbeth's gaze grew distant and she began to speak in a sing-song voice.

Below, below, far, far below
Go through and deeper still
Until the way is lost to you
Is destiny fulfilled

Jaxina shivered the words like a current of ice water drifting upon her skin. She jutted out her chin to hide her dread. "Well those are very vague directions."

Lorbeth cocked her head at Jaxina and rolled her eyes. "If it were easy, anyone would do it."

"But they don't even make sense. How does getting lost help you?"

"Are you scared?" Lorbeth said. "Well, you have to be brave. After all, only the most worthy can find the Umbra Orchid."

The two friends swam out into the wild places, through coral-sculpted grottos, past grinning moray eels and snapping crabs, and under the bellies of behemoths. They swam fast and far, until their familiar cerulean sea gave way to deep sapphire. Jaxina had long left behind any familiar landmarks, but Lorbeth guided them down toward a cool river of sea water flowing along the ocean floor. Ahead, the sea floor dropped off into a chasm.

"There," Lorbeth said, pointing over the edge. "We have to go down there."

Clear sapphire water filled the chasm but that was all, though it was large enough to hold a small pod of whales. In the centre lay a pool of water, the colour an indigo almost as dark as Jaxina's tail indicating a dramatic drop-off. Jaxina shivered. The pit looked like the pupil of a stern, disapproving eye staring up at her. She shuddered with fear as she backed away from the edge.

"That's the Giant's Gaze chasm. What are we doing here?"

"Where else would one find a rare flower?" Lorbeth said.

"But it is forbidden to enter." Jaxina looked back, her mind recalling the way they had travelled. Certainly she could trace her path back, if she needed to.

"Well, I'm going in," Lorbeth said, glaring at Jaxina.

She slid off the edge. Immediately the girl flipped top over tail, caught in an invisible current. Her body twisted and tumbled and then bounced against the rocky wall of the chasm with enough force to shake loose rocks. Lorbeth's arms flopped and her tail whipped back and forth in painful contortions as she tumbled down unconscious.

Jaxina launched herself off the ledge toward her friend. A vortex buffeted Jaxina's body. She gritted her teeth and locked her body tight until it flew through the water like a spear. Ahead, a watery tornado captured Lorbeth, spinning her deeper into the chasm. It swallowed her limp form and forced the girl inexorably toward the blackest centre of the hole.

With a powerful stroke, Jaxina drove forward and hit Lorbeth in the mid-section. They tumbled together in the swirling maelstrom, until Jaxina twisted free. She grasped Lorbeth's hands in hers and pulled her friend close, arms trembling with the effort. The tornado of water corkscrewed, plunging them deeper into the chasm.

Jaxina strained to keep them away from the rock face and in the center of the vortex. Jagged outcroppings jutted from the wall. If she let up for even an instant, the twisting current would hurl them against the walls where they would certainly be battered and shredded to pieces. Jaxina however could not fight the tide that sucked them down. Suddenly, they shot through the dark pupil of the Giant's Gaze and into darkness.

Around them the current eased. The dark water grew calm. Jaxina however, held her friend tightly, her heart beating like a tolling bell. She shook with fear and her muscles quivered from her exertions, but she did not let go of Lorbeth's limb body.

Jaxina blinked and stared into the black water, willing her heart to calm while she waited for her vision to adjust. Slowly her surroundings took shape, dark shadows rising against a glistening backdrop. They floated in a cavern. Black sand covered the floor below and shining obsidian walls on all sides

Lorbeth squirmed in Jaxina's arms and then shrugged free. "I'm fine. Just a little dizzy." She pointed at an opening in the wall. "We go through there."

"Wait," Jaxina said as she grabbed her friend. "Are you sure about this?"

With a scowl, Lorbeth yanked herself free. She swam ahead and in a few beats of her tail, disappeared.

Jaxina hugged herself as she squinted into the darkness. "Lorbeth?" A scream shot at her through the water. Lorbeth's scream.

Jaxina darted through the opening in the rock toward the sound of the scream. The dark amethyst waters around her surrendered to a sick yellow glow. Jaxina pulled up as she entered a cave, her tail flicking back and forth in fear.

Lorbeth floated in the middle of the space, trapped by what looked like ropes; variegated violet-colored ropes.

"Help me, Jaxina," Lorbeth said. She struggled as ropes wrapped themselves tighter around her arms and waist. "Help."

"Stop fighting."

"Easy for you to say," Lorbeth said, her voice hissing with desperate gasps of fear.

Jaxina breathed deeply, her gill flaps processing the water of the chamber, and sensed something curious about her surroundings. She stilled her tail and let the tide carry her closer Lorbeth.

"What are you doing?" Lorbeth said. "You want us both to be trapped?"

"Shush," Jaxina said. Her arm drifted upward. Jaxina let her fingers caress the tide flowing near the thickest rope, which was in fact not a rope at all but thick rubbery skin and tough sinew. It was a tentacle. They all were.

The thickest tentacle slithered and wrapped a coil around the end of Lorbeth's fin. Lorbeth's teal eyes grew wide with panic, but she remained still. Jaxina drifted closer and closer, blowing bubbles as she hummed. She crooned a calming warble, reaching out with sound and breath to touch the creature, just as she had with her anemone. This time however something reached back. Through the waves she felt the enormity of the creature; its strength, but also its sadness.

"When you're free," Jaxina said, as she focused on the tentacles, "don't move."

First, the one wrapped around Lorbeth's right arm released, then the one around her left. Finally, the last tentacle slid away from Lorbeth's fin. Together they floated freely. "Now. Just let the current take you."

The two mermaids were gently carried through a shell encrusted opening to a corridor made of more black stone.

"What was that?" Lorbeth asked swimming away.

"Amazing," Jaxina said, still caught in the immensity of the creature. "And sad. That poor thing trapped down here."

Lorbeth rolled her eyes and swam away toward a warm green light at the end of the passage. Jaxina sighed, trying to dispel the intense emotions, so much more than the feeble quiver from her anemone. She was so preoccupied; she almost swam up Lorbeth's back. Lorbeth slowly turned around to reveal a large bloom; a purple orchid. Eight long petals shaded from black to pale lilac, curled around a bright purple center.

"I found it. The Umbra Orchid," Lorbeth said. "I have to get back."

"Wait," Jaxina said. "What about me?"

"Rare means only one," Lorbeth said, backing away and with a sweep of her tail, she swam away, the single bloom clutched in her hand.

The way out was clear; a passage flushed by a very strong tide leading out to open water. But then what? The cavern was empty. There were no other flowers.

Tears from Jaxina's eyes mixed with the salty sea water. She flinched when she felt a touch on her hand. She looked down to find a tentacle touching her arm in a comforting caress. Then the tentacle waved in greeting.

It snaked away, and Jaxina followed the sinewy limb to a large cavern. The walls were covered in orchids. Camouflaged among them was a huge octopus creature. A pair of softly glowing eyes peered at her through the darkness of the space.

"I'm sure there's a way," Jaxina said. "You just have to find it."

"I have a story to offer," Jaxina said, as she stood before the gathering for the ceremony. "You see Lorbeth's flower." Lorbeth grinned and held up her offering. The mer-folk around her applauded. "I too journeyed. Below. Far, far, below, and through, and deeper still. Until I was lost. And only then did I find it."

A shadow floated over the gathering. Everyone looked up. Long, ropey tentacles spread out from the main body. They looked like variegated violet coloured petals wafting in the water. In the center, the bright purple bulk of the creature bulged. It drifted down toward the crowd. Mer-folk paled and backed away. Some floated, hands covering wide gaping mouths. There were not a few barely muffled screams.

Two luminous eyes searched the crowd. Finally, they fixed on Jaxina. Jaxina smiled and reached out to gently hold one twitching purple tentacle. "May I present the Umbra Orchid *Kraken.*" Another rubbery arm slithered out to pluck the orchid flower from Lorbeth's hand. "Oh. That's his food."

Ciminy swam toward her daughter, awe and joy written all over her face. She embraced Jaxina. "How?"

"I just had to find my way."

Thoughtful Young

The Highest Orange

Janka Hobbs

Once upon a time, high up in a tree, grew an orange. The tree lived in an orchard, where it received plenty of water and fertilizer, and, since the orange was at the top of the tree, it got lots of sunshine as well.

The orange looked around, and noticed that it was the one nearest the top of the tree. "I am the highest orange here," the orange told itself. "I must be the best."

It looked down at all the other oranges in the tree, and told them "I am the highest orange here. I get lots of sunshine, and it makes me very sweet. You should be more like me."

Most of the other oranges on the tree looked up, and thought, "You are lucky to be high up in the tree. We are doing the best we can on our own branches." But a few others said, "You are so big and juicy. We want to be more like you."

"Send me some of your sugar, and our tree will have the biggest, sweetest orange ever!" said the highest orange.

A few of the smaller oranges lower on the tree did so, even though they really had none to spare. Maybe they thought the big orange meant all the oranges on the tree would get sweeter.

The orange at the top of the tree got bigger and soaked up more and more of the water and nutrients that flowed through its branch.

When the highest orange noticed there were oranges on its tree that had not sent it any sugar, it told everyone who would listen "Oranges that do not send their sugar to the top of the tree are selfish and don't even care about making our tree the best tree!"

Some of the oranges that heard this became angry, but the words made a few of the others feel bad, and those sent some of their sugar to the top of the tree.

The orange at the top of the tree got even bigger, and soaked up even more of the water and nutrients that flowed through its branch. It looked around and said, "I am the biggest, sweetest orange in the whole orchard!"

But then it noticed that there were still some oranges on the tree that had not sent it any sugar, and it became angry. "How can I become the biggest, sweetest orange ever, if there are still oranges on this tree that will not send me any sugar?"

Just then, a bug flew by. "Bug!" called the orange. "You will help me! Bring me sugar from those other oranges!"

The bug buzzed around the orange for a while. It smelled how sweet and ripe the orange was. The bug was looking for a place to lay its eggs, and it thought, "This would be a good place for my maggots to grow." The bug said to the orange, "I will bring you sugar from the other oranges, but I will have to poke a tiny hole in your skin to send it in."

The orange thought about this. It did not like the idea of a hole in its beautiful orange skin. But the bug promised it would be a very tiny hole, and promised it would bring the orange lots more sugar. And when the highest orange thought about the oranges on the tree that had not sent any sugar, it decided it had no choice. "Go bring me sugar from those other selfish oranges!" the highest orange ordered.

The bug flew off, and circled around the tree. It was surprised at how small and sour the other oranges on the tree were, but it did find a few that still had enough sugar to be edible. It buzzed around, found the best of these, took a bite, and sucked out some juice. Then it flew back to the orange at the top of the tree, drilled a hole in its side, and deposited five hundred and forty-three eggs.

"Ooh, I can feel myself growing!" said the highest orange. "I am the biggest, sweetest orange ever!"

The bug flew away, satisfied that its maggots would be happy.

A few days later, there was a storm. The wind came up, and bent the tree's branches to and fro. The highest orange was tossed back and forth and up and down. It was so big and juicy, and weighed so much, that the branch it was on broke.

"Why didn't you make my branch stronger?" the no-longer-highest orange yelled as it tumbled past the other oranges.

"We sent you all the sugar!" they yelled back, but it was too late.

The no-longer-highest orange landed with a thump on the ground under the tree. Pulp and orange juice and maggots splattered in all directions.

After the storm, the orchardists came out to clean up the mess. They were dismayed to see all the larvae crawling in the pulp, and quickly scooped them up so they would not spread to the other trees. They also wondered why all the remaining oranges on the tree looked so small and sour. "Whatever could have happened here?" they thought. "I hope it doesn't happen again."

Thoughtful Young

Minnox the Hunter

Jillian Sulliven

When Olga's fortune went, she was given a rough planked hut on the edge of her old estate in which to live.

The new owner, Lenonsky, rode a dappled grey stallion through the forests to her door.

"Old woman," he called to her, not Madame, not even Olga anymore. "If you will sweep the leaves from the driveway every day, I will give you a reward."

Olga came to stand on her doorstep.

"Huh. Will you give me back my home?" she said.

"No, but there will be wood and wine and food for you when the winter comes."

"Keep your wood. What is mine is mine and forever will be." Her earrings caught the sun and blazed.

"You will regret turning down my kindness when the snow lies deep."

"My dignity will keep me warm. I won't bend my back for you," said Olga.

When he left, Olga lit the stove inside her hut. She had wood. She would find more. She fed the twigs into the black stove's open mouth.

All Olga had kept of her fortune, her finery, were the blue jewels at her ears. These she wore every day, putting them in in the morning when the sun rose in the grey sky and her fingers creaked in the cold. She took the jewels out each night to lie in a box by her bed. When she looked at her earrings, she remembered everything: her jewels, her clothes, her dazzling life.

One night a cat, black and pitiful and thin, crept out of the forest and came to Olga's door. Olga shared her rough bread and stew with it, and when the cat settled down in front of the fire, Olga thought about herself and the cat. I am like a witch in a fairy book now, she thought, when really I

103

am a queen. Still, she smiled to herself to think of Lenonsky riding his Arab stallion through the woods, thinking he was safe, thinking he was lord of all, when on the edge of his universe there lived a witch with her black cat.

It's like a story, Olga thought. Yet in the morning when she looked in her cupboard which was now one shelf bare of food, she thought how there was an extra mouth to feed and the crack of winter almost upon them.

In her old life, with her feather bed and her maid to make it and a cook and a man to open the door, a little scrawny cat such as this would not have existed. Olga had had animals of course; she'd had her own black stallion, sleek and fit with painted hooves and soft eyes. Her own stallion was sold now. The grey Arab stallion now in his place.

Still, sharing her porridge, her bread and her stew, Olga liked to see the covering of fat grow upon the cat and its fur lie against its skin, shining like the stallion's did, and the cat's graceful leap onto her knees. Lenonsky rode through the forest to the village and didn't call past her hut. He left Olga to burn the last of her wood pile and eat the last of her food. When he thought the cold and hunger had brought down her pride, he rode up to her hut again.

He had a fine life, living in Olga's palace. He had sumptuous food and a fit horse between his legs. What he wanted was to see Olga raking up leaves for him. Who cared if the wind took the piles and scattered them? The sight of Olga, back bent, working for him on land that was once hers, he thought, would finally let him know that it was he who had power in this land–Lenonsky the Lord, not Olga the Queen.

When he rode up to the hut with the cold air crackling around his ears and his hands warm inside his muff, he saw through the window Olga cooking at the fire. There were still twigs she had found then, and the carcass on the table was a rabbit's.

How is she able to hunt? he thought. *She is worn and old.* He did not see the cat crouched in the shadow of the room. Minnox the Hunter, Olga called the cat. Once it was she who had saved and fed the cat, and now it was the cat who hunted for both of them.

The fire burned merrily, but it was Olga's chair she burned for warmth, not logs–and what she had left to burn was her table and her bed and the little box for the earrings, and then, only the planks of the hut.

There were the earrings she could sell for wood, but Olga would not do this. She stirred the pot at the stove, grateful for the warmth from her chair, and thought of the stew to come and of how Minnox's eyes shone in the light of the fire, like jewels in the shadow of the room. *Like the jewel in my ear*, she thought.

She didn't see behind her the window with the snowflakes pattering down, their silent fall covering the tracks of Lenonsky and his horse as he made his way home to the palace.

The next day, he rode past again. *Where is she hunting? And where is she finding the wood?* He halted his stallion and watched Olga make her way from the hut, through the trees and on to the wide driveway that leads up to his palace.

She is coming to beg my mercy, he thought, and smiled upon his stallion, man and horse breathing white air into the sky.

Olga stooped, bent over, her hands moved through the leaves turning them and pushing them aside.

Ahh, she is sweeping the drive for me already, Lenonsky thought, *with her bare hands, her old back faced to the sky.* He turned his horse and cantered home to wait for her arrival.

Olga did not come. She turned and turned the leaves on the drive until at last she found the blue jeweled earring she'd lost the night before as she searched for twigs, for anything dry to light her fire.

The earring found, she turned back to her hut, woodless, and Minnox returned home also, rabbitless.

When Lenonsky rode by that evening he saw in the grey shelter of the hut, Olga standing by the dark unlit stove, no food on the table.

She had thought to burn her bed, but with no food as a reward, she had decided to stay cold instead. Only Minnox in the shadows saw the man on his horse stare, then ride away.

When Lenonsky got home to his palace with the huge fire burning in the hall, and the long table set with steaming bowls of food, he thought of how the old woman had worked for him on the driveway and not even asked for her reward but gone home instead to stand in a cold, unlit hut.

Lenonsky leaned forward to put another thick log on his fire. Sparks cracked and danced. He held his hands out to the orange warmth.

I am warm and she is cold, he thought. *I am well fed, my stomach strains against my trousers. I have eaten meats and rich dark bread and sugared fruit and drunk a good bottle of red wine. Soon I will go to my feathered bed which was once hers.*

He held his hands to the flames waiting for the joy his thoughts should bring him. Instead he saw Olga in his mind, turning and shifting his leaves, and Olga in her dark cold hut, and this wasn't what he wanted to imagine. He wanted to look forward to her bed and the fine linen sheets. "Mine, mine," he said out loud.

His fingers felt chilled, though he held them to the flames. The fire could not warm his memory. He saw once more in his mind his own fingers gloveless and iced over and his too-small boots, cracked and split in the snow, and Olga's father, the Lord, as his hand arced up with the whip.

No. Lenonsky pushed back his chair and stood up. His wolfhound rose with him.

"I am Lenonsky the Lord now," he shouted so even the flagstones in the great hall would know he had spoken. "She is nothing. She is not fit to even be my servant."

He went up the stone steps to his bed chamber where the fire was lit and the bed heaped warm with her furs.

That night he dreamt of Olga, and it was she who was young now and cowered at her father's whip. The dream woke him; he felt again the lancing pain of the cord on his skinny back.

Olga woke in the grey snowlight of a snowing day. Minnox was at the door, eager to get out and hunt. She was losing her summer fat, Olga saw. She would soon be again the pitiful thin cat that Olga had found.

"Out you go then, and may luck be with you." Olga pulled the wooden door closed again, though it was just as cold in as out.

Today then, I will sell one earring. One, she thought. For how could she let Minnox starve, when Minnox had saved her up till then?

She went to her bed and took the box with the blue jeweled earrings and she put one in her ear and one in her pocket, pulled her shawl up over her hair and went out into the white and the cold.

Lenonsky saw her as he rode by. He saw her stop at his driveway and look up towards the palace, and not even with longing, he saw, or defiance, or any need but the need to keep moving, how the sleet rushed into her face and her chest. She walked towards his home.

"Olga," he called her. She turned and saw him on his stallion, a grey horse under a grey sky, and coal black eyes. She wished the horse would breathe its warm breath into her face and went towards them.

Lenonsky watched her walk towards him and his heart remembered his fire last night and how in the end it couldn't warm the memory from his bones.

"I have wine and furs for you," he said. "And food I have no need for."

She lifted her hand toward him and opened her fingers to show the sky-blue jewel.

"For this," she said and held her hand open.

"No. For you," he said, and looked at the blue stone, how it flashed without the sun to shine at it.

"Keep it," he said. "I have enough." And his skin suddenly warmed and flamed inside his jacket and boots and gloves.

He found a room for her in the palace, and a bed and a fire. He brought her very own sheets.

She brought with her Minnox, who grew fat and sleek again on castle mice and castle food.

She wore her earrings but not her finest clothing. She sat by the fire at night and anyone looking in the window would not know—was she the Lady or he the Lord? For they were both warmed by the flames and content to be so.

Minnox favoured both laps with her trusting warmth. The flames blazed light across their faces and the earrings flashed their pale brilliance into the room.

The hut in the woods dissolved back into the earth, plank by plank, and was covered, like memories, with the forgiveness of snow.

Fairy Rosieo and St. Julian

Donna J. W. Munro

Once upon a time, Fairy Rosieo minded all of the flowers in the monastery garden. Her red hair, bright as blood and curled like breaths of spring wind, gave rise her name. It was whispered that the King of the fairies so loved her beauty that he made roses in her honor. Others said the rose's thorns were the retribution of the fairy queen, jealous of the young fairy's beauty.

What others say often only tells the story of the powerful and Fairy Rosieo had little power beyond her garden. But that bothered her not, for she loved her garden, for it was life itself.

She made things grow. Her patch of earth smiled under the afternoon sun of spring, dotted with wreaths of flowers for fairy dancing, hedges of bright yellow heather, and the most perfect tear shaped rosebuds of the deepest red. Humans wandered through the garden, watering, seeding, thinking that they made the garden so lush. Their huge feet crushed the bluebells that bloomed under her ministering touch. Their hands plucked her babies into clutches of decapitated buds for their lovers.

Snipping. Nipping. Tearing. Ripping.

Each attack of human admiration made Fairy Rosieo weep.

Until one day, a young monk with wide brown eyes knelt gently beside her rosebushes. With simple tools, he worked the remains of the mash the monks had eaten for lunch into the soil. The lush scents of nutrients folding into moist earth made her pause in her work. She floated behind a pointed leaf, watching him. She'd seen humans work with her flowers, but never with such care. And he sang. Words and tones so sweet poured from him, but in whispered song. Nothing showy. Not like the men who dragged giggling girls into the fairy circles, trampling the bright spots of color as they clutched each other in fevered lust. He loved her garden near as much as she.

Every day he worked the flowers, killing the pests that ate the leaves, cutting away dead branches, and pulling the crowding weeds that strangled the flower's roots. She watched him work and fell in love. So much stood between them. His vows. Her size. His Christian denial of her existence.

"I love you," she whispered while he sang his song. She flitted after him, dropping her magic on the blooms he tended, charming them taller, pushing the petals out in perfect rings. Of course, he couldn't hear. He praised his God for each garden miracle he found. It was enough to hear his voice speak of the beauty she'd made for him, even if he didn't know. She followed him for years, working by his side in the garden. She wondered if he would ever notice the flash of her wings or hear her voice singing the words of his hymns in gentle harmony.

Cracks appeared in his face. His thin fingers' skin faded like rice paper, letting the blue veins show. He moved more slowly. Sometimes boys helped him get back to his feet after kneeling to weed. Still, his voice whispered songs the way she'd always loved. Sometimes he'd stop and listen to the sounds of the green, leaning back and wiping his forehead on his wide sleeve. Then she'd fly to his ears, buzzing and singing her own song of love. She made promises to love only him, forever. She begged him to follow her into her fairy circles where she might save him from aging, pain, and death. In those silences, he would smile and wipe away the sweat dotting his lip with his scratchy sleeve.

When he'd lived sixty-eight summers, a goodly old man, he made to rise from kneeling and fell. She fussed and worried since no other human saw the fall. He panted there, laying half out of a fairy circle. She flew around his head, crying out, cursing her size.

"Now, now," he said. "Settle down lady fairy." The breath of the monk came slower and she heard the rattle of something broken in his chest.

She landed on his wrinkled cheek, stroking his face and crying—a soft noise lost to all but him.

"You hear me?"

The monk nodded. "I've always heard. Your beautiful voice, your wonders have all been kindnesses. Temptations I've resisted. I go to my maker with a clean soul. I've not been led astray by your beauty, but oh little fairy I sang of you every day."

"Let me save you, my love. Let me bring you to the bright hill where you'll never die. I can't make you young, but I'll keep you alive. You've earned a rest with me, love."

The monk smiled again as she flew in front of his eyes. Her boldness shocked her. What would the king and queen of her fairy hill think of her bringing him? She didn't care, so much did she love him.

"No dear little fairy. I must keep my vow and go to my God. My life has been one of beauty, thanks to you and our work. A purer, truer love never existed."

She fluttered before his eyes, rising and falling on the warmth of his breath, listening to the thready beat of his heart. The pulses slowed with each breath until soon only one breath remained. It flowed out and his gaze distanced. His thin skin plumped as the light of God passed over his aged features. She threw herself into that light, though it burned.

"I will not let him leave me!" She screamed. "Take me too."

The beam moved away, rejecting her plea.

oOo

The monks found him, covered in the petals of the flowers he'd grown. At his funeral, a song filled the rafters of the church with words no one had ever heard and melodies of another place. They buried him, not in the monks' graveyard, but in the garden. The face of his grave grew blankets of roses every year. Every other plant in the garden died.

His marker calls him a saint for the miracles surrounding his death.

Saint Julian.

Upon the stone, some poet chipped, *A glooming peace this morning brings; The sun, for sorrow, will not show his head.*

To this day, the roses weep.

The Pink Parking Lot Patrol

Karin Frank

"Now get under the covers. Pull them up to your chin and close your eyes.

"Good. Good. Now Mommy will tell you a story about her Mommy. Close your eyes. Good. Good.

"This all happened back in the day when people first realized the planet was

warming so much that our very civilization was in danger. People who worried about it and wanted to do something were willing to try anything. And your Gramma was one of those people.

"I'll tell it just like a story that you can read on your tablet. And I'll keep talking until you get really drowsy and can fall asleep."

oOo

"You are not going to spread that black bitumen over this surface," the frail-looking old lady in the pink pussycat hat said to the burly construction worker in the yellow hard hat.

The summer sun beat down on both their heads.

Pee sizzled on the emptied parking lot where a dog had just whizzed. The air right above wavered.

A few children who had nowhere else to play and a handful of stray dogs looking for a handout had been taken elsewhere. Both had been eager to leave the sweltering pavement for promises of playground and food.

"Parking lots have always been asphalt," the boss hardhat said. "Parking lots have always been black." He towered over the lady's gray head.

But she managed somehow to go up on her tiptoes so she could get up in his face. Where the top of her head could not reach, her pointing finger could. "Times they are a'changing,'" she quoted a song from her childhood. "Get with it." The little pink ears of her beanie waggled as she shook her head at him.

"Don't get mad at me, Granny." He backed off a half step or two. "I'm just doing my job."

"And we know who pays you, Sonny," said one of the other six people, four women and two men, arrayed behind her. Gray hairs poked out from their pink pussycat caps as well.

The hardhat scowled at the two men wearing pink pussycat hats. But those venerable old gentlemen replied with broad grins and knowing nods. "Don't think your hardhat makes you more of a man than I am," one of them said. "My beanie's crocheted out of metallic fiber." He chuckled.

"It's pink," the hardhat said as though that said it all.

"And yours is yellow," the other gentleman said in a somewhat belligerent tone.

They seemed about to come to blows about the underlying meaning of colors.

"Boys, boys, boys," the granny-in-charge commanded. "Grow up."

After some huffing and puffing, they stuffed fists into pockets and exchanged sheepish grins.

"Was he the bad guy?

"No, dear, he was just a worker earning a paycheck to feed his family, like Mommy. Like you soon will be. But one of the bad guys did show up."

"A suit?"

"A suit."

A huge silver limo pulled up to the curb. Nothing could be seen through the opaqued and bullet-proofed windows but workers and protesters knew who rode inside.

One of the doors opened and three Cavalier King Charles Spaniels bounced out. The dogs made for the sun-browned verges of the lot to relieve themselves. They seemed to prance regally across the asphalt lifting their paws high and placing them spritely, but whimpers revealed their capering was due to the pain from the blistering pavement.

A man followed. He wore Ray Bans and Armani.

"What are those things, Mommy?"

"Those are brand names for expensive sunglasses and a very expensive tailored suit. Wealthy people once cherished such things. They considered them to be marks of their personal worth."

"But that's just stuff."

"Yup, stuff. But stuff was once thought to be more important than people."

"Oh, that's sicko."

"Yes, sweetie, sicko."

The man stepped between the hardhat and the pink hats. He sneered at everyone.

"Asphalt company representative," the hardhat whispered.

Granny nodded to him. "Tied to petroleum. Enemy of the people."

She turned to her crew and jerked her chin in the newcomer's direction. "Represents big oil, the folks who got us in this mess."

The members of her crew growled softly, their pink hats bobbing.

"Grannies." The epithet appeared to leave a bad taste in the suit's mouth. He seemed to spit his next words. "What do you think you can accomplish, stopping these men from working, standing up to me? I can have you all disappeared with the wave of my hand." He raised his arm and seemed to be about to wave them away.

The hardhat shuddered.

"And we will be replaced immediately by others," said Granny. "Our numbers are infinite. We seven may be activists but we represent the masses. We're the climate change brigades. Once we were known as Red Hat Societies and Silver Sneakers Health Clubs. Now we are known as the Pink Parking Lot Patrols. At the moment, I speak for all."

"The suit laughed. The climate change brigade? I only see a few specks of lint." He flicked dismissive fingers along the shoulders of his suit.

The hardhat flinched.

Spokesgranny leaned slightly to one side and inclined her head at him. "He includes you in that," she said.

The hardhat nodded but he kept his mouth shut.

"We are the oil magnates," the suit snarled, using the royal 'we' he felt was his right.

"Previous governments have allowed us massive tax breaks. Previous governments have fought wars to protect our interests. We're not going to fade into the shadows meekly. Our hold on economies remains tenacious."

Spokesgranny straightened and peered directly into the darkened lenses of his sunglasses. She barely came up to his shoulders but her small bulk was enough to intrude on his personal space.

"We intend to spend our retirement days," she declared, "painting and repaving parking lots pink. Decades ago Berkeley City Planners in California experimented with pastel parking lots. They discovered the lighter surfaces ran 40 degrees cooler than the surrounding blacktop. Since then, we've made it our mission to make the world's parking lots pink."

He held back her speech with the splayed fingers of his outstretched hand. but she spoke from behind that barrier as though it didn't exist. "Your kind will die out," she declared with a deadly softness. An aplomb developed over millennia of human evolution gave these words the strength of ancient rocks.

This time, the suit flinched. He tried to respond as though he were still in command, but his words were hesitant. "Your—your statement borders on the fanatical," he stuttered. "I find that somewhat unnerving."

"You should. Not because I am a zealot but because you know the wheels of history will roll right over you."

He glared down at her as though he wanted to kill her right then and there.

"And to help those wheels along," she continued whipping a folded piece of paper out of her overalls. "I have here an order from the Department of the Interior." She spread the paper out and waved it like a battle flag in his face.

"The government in D.C. has declared this parking lot will join the ranks of fighters against climate change.

Equipment will arrive shortly to repave this surface with a pastel aggregate that reflects sunlight."

She handed it to him. "Read it and weep."

"Who slipped this through?" He asked rhetorically, no longer looking anyone in the eye.

She answered him with facts, "Others of my kind." She nodded with satisfaction. "The people have voted new voices into office."

Growling, the master of fossil fuels turned on his heels, his relieved spaniels dancing at his feet, and strode back to his limo.

"We're going to fill in all your potholes pink," yelled one of the gentlemen in a pink pussy hat and gave him the thumbs up with both hands.

The hardhat sniggered. "Well," he said. "I guess I'm through here."

Spokesgranny smiled. "Let's get to work guys." she called to her crew.

oOo

Yawn. "What happened then?"

"Well, a few days after the pale pink aggregate dried, the temperature over the parking lot dropped forty degrees under the broiling sun. Children tossed balls back and forth. Dogs pranced without pain as their humans walked them to the water-absorbent verges.

"This, my child, was one of the first encounters between those mired in the old ways and the masters of the new.

"Now climate change brigades make their way across the continents. They paint and repave one parking lot, one highway, at a time to help preserve civilization for their grandchildren.

"Remember, sleepy head, your Gramma was one of those people that helped save the world we have. So now, you can lie in your own cozy bed and go to sleep and know that everything is going to be okay."

Thoughtful Young

Dragon Language

Rob G. Bachman

Even the comforting sunset, descending upon the remote little village of Erdemor like a velvet blanket, couldn't distract young Erdwin from his knowledge that the dragons would return the very next day.

It should have been on everyone's calendar, but no one wanted to talk about it.

The townspeople didn't seem to care when he tried to warn them; going about their business as if it weren't the Third Day of Spring. They tended the vegetable crops in the gardens, fed their livestock, repaired cracks in aging wooden houses, and fetched water from the spring near Dire Mountain as if it were any other day.

Maybe there IS a little more hustle and bustle, thought Erdwin, trying to convince himself as he poured the last round of mash from his bucket into the pigs' feeding trough. Their pen was just a short walk across the street from his house, next to the clearing at the edge of town, under the old Gronta tree. The half-dozen swine anxiously approached him for their dinner, good-naturedly grunting and oinking, pushing each other aside for his attention. After they were fed, Erdwin addressed them all individually by name.

"Good night Emma, Irma, Hank, Snoops, Durwin, and Rog," he said.

It was probably not a good idea to name the animals, since—as his father Torbin constantly reminded him—they would all eventually be food, but Erdwin had done so anyway. Friends all, his pigs were. Especially Rog, who was his favorite. It seemed like they could actually understand each other sometimes.

He hoped he would be able to keep them safe when the dragons came.

Erdwin had never seen a dragon, except for tales and drawings in dusty old books. According to legend the creatures only returned once every thousand years. There was no way to be sure, but going by what he'd read, it would be *this year*, on the Fourth day of Spring. It had been on his mind almost every waking minute the past few days.

"So, were they hungry?" his mother, Eline, asked. Erdwin was startled and surprised to find himself inside the house. He'd been too lost in thought to realize he'd walked in the door. Eline was busy cleaning pots and pans next to the wood stove.

"The dragons?" Erdwin blurted, closing the rickety door.

"No, silly, the pigs," his mother said.

"Oh, sure. They're always hungry."

Erdwin plunked down on one of the big cushions near the window. He spent a lot of time reading, sitting here in his favorite place. The thought of not being able to do that anymore—if the dragons burned down their house, or worse—made him sad and afraid at the same time.

"You know, Mum," he said, "the dragons are coming back tomorrow. We need to get ready to escape."

"Oh, not again, Erdwin," his mother sighed. She put away her cooking items and sat down next to him. "Stop worrying about that. It's going to be okay. The dragons aren't really coming back. It's just...mythology. Fairy tales and such."

"But those books I read...the ones from the library at the Citadel. They all say the dragons will come out of the caves in Dire Mountain and burn everything in their path. We're the closest town, Mum! They'll get us first!"

Eline put her hand on her son's shoulder. "If they do come, we will escape. There's always the root cellar behind the house. We've got room in there for at least half of the townspeople, if need be."

"But there might not be time," Erdwin said.

"Well, then you'll just have to try talking them out of it," his mother said with a wink.

Erdwin's sadness turned to curiosity. "How did you know I was studying Dragon Language?"

"Your teacher, Sir Platch. He thought it funny you would even want to read those musty old tomes. They have to be at least a hundred years old."

"The books are more than a thousand years old, Mum. Can you believe it? When they were written, people actually talked to dragons!" Erdwin grew excited. Finally, someone might listen to him. "I thought maybe I could talk to them too. I learned how the language works and how to say basic things. It's mostly burps and squeaks and gross noises. But people can make the sounds, and maybe if I talk to them they won't..."

"That's a nice thought, Erdwin. But don't drive yourself crazy with all these old stories. You're twelve years old, not a hundred and twelve. Stop worrying about the dragons. Everything will be fine." Eline smiled, patted his shoulder again, and got up.

Erdwin sighed, and out of frustration tried speaking a few Dragon phrases out loud. "Errrg....brap," he said. This meant 'hello'. "Bzzzz....fargenor" was 'good day'. And his favorite was "Pfft....poot....eerrp....ferrrrt ack!" which translated to "please don't eat us!"

He had learned that phrase first.

The next day, the dragons came.

There were four of them, each at least 50 feet long, giant wings flapping, screaming out from the backside of Dire Mountain and darkening the midmorning skies over the village. Townspeople ran in every direction along the main street, seeking shelter among trees or in bushes. Some headed for the nearby hills.

Torbin was out on the porch of the little house. He tugged nervously at his beard. One of the dragons flew past, a blur of leathery wings and scales, and the next instant a house down the street burst into flames.

Erdwin, who a few minutes ago was enjoying a nice breakfast, ran outside and cried, "I tried to tell you, Father! No one listened to me!"

"Yes, you did,but that's not important right now. We need to get to the cellar," Torbin said. "It's our only chance!"

Now there were a few people running toward his house, seeking shelter. Erdwin noticed Karl the blacksmith, his wife, their teenage son Jimny, and Dorgan, the town alchemist. Eline ran out of the house and joined them, her face painted with worry.

A dragon landed with a THUMP! in the clearing, near the animal pen, sending great plumes of dust into the air. Erdwin's pigs made an awful ruckus as they tried in vain to escape. Somewhere, there was the sound of a house collapsing, and a woman's scream.

At Tobin's urging, everyone hurried under the stoop.

"They burned down my barn! What are we going to do?" asked Karl, the blacksmith.

The dragon stomped around, leaving deep footprints in the ground as it neared the animals.

"Can't get to the cellar now," said Torbin. "That dragon is too close. It could pick us off one by one." The beast sniffed at the pigpen, and then turned to face the villagers.

"We're cut off," Torbin added, and looked at his son gravely.

"I might be able to help," Erdwin said. No one else had a better idea, so he had to try. "I've been studying the ancient Dragon Language."

"Oh please, son, this isn't the time for that silliness," Torbin said.

Erdwin frowned. "Maybe it *is* a stupid idea. But what else can we do?"

His father started to say something, then was silent.

"He does have a point, you know," said Dorgan, the alchemist.

Another dragon landed in the clearing. Then another. Finally, the fourth, and largest, swooped to the ground in front of its brethren. This was obviously their leader: it had thick, greenish brown skin, with huge scales the size of shields covering its body. A row of spikes lined its back, some at least ten feet in length. Its enormous eyes were like a cat's, the iris yellow and the pupil a thin black slit. It glared at the small group of frightened villagers as it sniffed at the air.

The entire village of Erdemor grew deathly silent. Even the pigs were quiet and had lined up attentively at the edge of their pen. They looked right at Erdwin, as if asking him for help.

Erdwin thought about the pigs, who were his responsibility, and his family and friends, who were now being threatened. He knew what he had to do, despite his father's doubts. He crawled out from under the stoop and walked into the street in front of his home, toward the clearing, only a few yards from the invading clan of monstrous beasts.

"Erdwin, don't!" Eline pleaded and started after her son.

Torbin stopped her. "Let him try," he said. "It might be our only chance."

The dragon leader roared, showing teeth like white swords, its tongue a giant forked snake. It blew a stream of fire into the air that seemed to touch the sun.

Erdwin held his ground.

The dragon stared at him.

He stared back.

The townspeople stared at Erdwin.

The pigs stared at the townspeople, then Erdwin, then the dragons.

Everyone waited.

And waited.

Smoke drifted down the street from a burning house.

Erdwin opened his mouth to speak, but he had forgotten the Dragon language words!

"Pfft..." he started. He couldn't remember what came next!

The dragons all cocked their heads in unison, listening.

Think, Erdwin, think! But nothing came to him. No words at all.

And at that moment, his stomach grumbled loudly, and he involuntarily burped. He had, after all, just had breakfast. Coincidentally, it sounded just like "Errrg....brap!", which was Dragon language for "hello."

"Errrg...brap!" the dragon replied, in a voice so loud it sent shingles flying off the roof of the house.

"Bzzzz....uh...fargenor!" Erdwin said haltingly. It was coming back to him now.

"Bzzzz....FARGENOR!" screeched the dragon. Its breath was so bad, leaves flew off the Gronta tree.

"Pfft....poot....eerrp....ferrrrt ack!" Erdwin shouted. This was Dragon Language for, "Please don't eat us!" Then he repeated it, for good measure, to make sure he got it right. A misunderstanding could make things worse. "Pfft....poot...eerrp...ferrrrt ack!"

The dragons all looked at each other, momentarily confused. The leader shook its head up and down in an almost humanlike gesture. "Urp aaaaaah grrrrrrr dzzzzzzz...." it roared, and suddenly all of the dragons took to the skies together, creating a great gust of wind as they flew away. A few wooden planks and shingles blew off the nearby houses. No one complained.

Everyone was silent for a moment, just to be safe, unmoving as they watched the dragons fade into the distance. They came out from their hiding place as Erdwin returned to the house. Finally, Dorgan said, "I guess all that studying paid off, young man."

"I guess it did," replied Erdwin. He was surprised that his plan actually worked. His mother hugged him.

"Nice work, son," said Torbin, and patted Erdwin on the back.

The blacksmith's son Jimny cleared his throat to get Erdwin's attention. "I was wondering," he asked in his high-pitched, screechy voice, "What did the dragon say to you, before they left?"

"It was pretty simple," replied Erdwin. "The dragon said, 'Why didn't you say so?'."

It took a while for life to get back to normal in the village, but day-by-day, it did. Six houses and the blacksmith's barn had been lost, burned by dragon fire, but everyone pitched in to help rebuild. Thanks to Erdwin, no humans or animals were eaten by dragons.

Where the creatures had gone, no one knew.

Sadly, on the Twentieth day of Spring, it was time for one of the pigs to go to market. Torbin had told him long ago that this would be a decision he would have to make, and Erdwin had agreed, thinking it was a day that would never come.

He trudged out to the pigpen. It was a dreary, rainy morning. Despite the foul weather, all six pigs eagerly ran to see him, curly tails wagging. It broke Erdwin's heart to have to decide which one to give up. Closing his eyes, he tried to pick blindly by pointing at the pigs, but they kept shuffling around and out of the way. Eventually the animals stopped moving, and his finger settled. He opened his eyes.

He had chosen his favorite friend. His finger pointed at Rog.

The pig startled him with a loud OINK! and seemed agitated, as if he could read his mind. He pawed at the crossbeams of the pen, and stamped his feet in the mud, refusing to look at Erdwin.

"What is it, Rog?" Tears welled up in Erdwin's eyes.

The pig looked directly at him, brown eyes pleading.

"Pfft....poot....eerrp....ferrrrt ack!" grunted Rog. He turned to look at his brothers and sisters in the pen, then back at Erdwin.

Rog had, after all, heard the entire conversation with the dragon.

Erdwin smiled, and patted the pig on his head. He had an idea. He would promise his father to plant many more vegetables this season, so long as Rog and the others were safe. Because they were, as one might say in Dragon Language, his "Aaar Baaz."

Friends.

"Urp aaaaaah grrrrrrr dzzzzzzz!" Erdwin said, in his best dragon voice, loud enough for the entire village to hear. Then he laughed and laughed as the overjoyed Rog spun in circles.

Thoughtful Young

On the Other Side of the Sky

Han Adcock

"Tell me a story, Babcia," Piotr said, his big hazel eyes peeking from the top of the blankets.

"What about?" Piotr's grandmother brushed the mess of black tendrils out of his eyes. He would need a haircut soon, once things had settled down.

"You could tell me what Mum and Dad are doing. Are they coming back from holiday yet?"

She hesitated. She wasn't ready to make that story yet. Telling the truth can be hard.

"How about I tell you the story of the Sun and the Moon?"

"You've not told that before."

"Rather silly of me not to, isn't it? Seeing as it's the tale of how everything began. Shall I?"

Piotr nodded.

"First there was the darkness of night, and there were the stars. There were so many stars, all clustered together, the darkness was hardly dark at all, but a black and white painting by Jackson Pollock. All that was, was sky—"

"Who's Jackson Pollock?"

Babcia looked at her eight-year-old grandson and hid a smile. Sometimes, he listened so well she forgot who she was talking to, until he coughed up a question like that.

"He was an artist who painted with dots and splashes."

"Oh."

"All there was, was sky...and the world below was only dirt. Under the dirt, deep, deep down, all the plants slept like babies, curled up green and close-leafed. The dirt was hard because it was dry rock. There weren't any clouds, just rock, darkness, and stars. It was cold and quiet and lonely, like this house becomes when my children or grandchildren are not staying here.

"The stars were small children. They had no mother or father, and they didn't know what they were doing there or why they had come into life."

"Were they sad?"

"No, because they had each other. They were far away, on the other side of the sky, casting light through their tiny peep holes so they could watch what happened to the world. They were curious.

"Nothing happened for a long time until Mother Moon came around the side of the world. She painted everything with shades of blue and silver, and blessed her star children, because although she may not have birthed them, they were hers to look after. She spent a lot of time with them, explaining what was going to happen.

"There will be a force from me soon," she said, "which will pull water towards me and push it away to the world below. Using this magic, I shall make a rain from you all."

"Why?" the youngest star said.

"It is part of the Universe's pattern. I have done this many times, for many other worlds. It is this world's time to feel the rain."

She concentrated, and beads of water flew from the stars' faces, carried along with bits of stardust. The moon gathered this together and let it fall to the world as the first rain. It rained until the world filled with glittering water, like a big cup, which then started to muddy as it broke down the harsh rocks and turned them into kind dirt.

The green babies sleeping under the ground stirred and drank the water, but still they did not wake up. Then, tired from the making of the rain, the stars and the Moon slept.

A beautiful, burning light woke them. The light was as golden as lions' eyes and amber as tigers' skin, and redder than a fire. It rose on the far horizon of the new world and turned to face them.

The light was a beautiful face, so strong and proud and almost too powerful for the stars to peep at, but the Moon could not help looking, and she caught a little of his light for herself. It filled her with warmth and life and wonder.

"What is happening here?" the light said, gazing angrily and haughtily upon the flooded world below. "You have wet the world right through! And why, lady, have you stolen some of my light?"

The Moon blushed purple-grey in some places and whispered that she loved the sight of him so much, she had to take a little from him to keep herself warm.

"It's the first time I ever felt warm," she said. "I never want to forget it. Who are you?"

The light softened when he saw himself reflected in her face.

"I am the Sun," he said.

So vain was he, he convinced both of them he loved her just as much as she loved him.

They sat side by side for many epochs, watching and playing with the world. He cooked the water so it rose into the sky, making clouds which spat the rain down again. The Moon played at rocking the waters back and forth, until the flood gave way to the land.

Then the green babies of the Moon and the Sun were born, pushing out from the ground, and they blossomed into a garden that covered the whole world.

The bits of stardust in the Moon's first rain settled onto the new land like a heron on a lake. The dust coalesced into tiny creatures with golden wings, quick minds, and a language of their own—"

"Fairies?" Piotr asked.

"If you like to call them that, then by all means, do so," Babcia said. "These creatures branched out and became the people of the land. Some of them lived in the sea as singing, silver fish-people, and some of them lived in the trees as tiny dragonfly-people. All was going so well."

She paused, unsure what to say next, remembering the raised voices and awkward atmosphere Piotr had seen and heard when living with his Mum and Dad before they had gone on holiday to try and find the love they had for each other again, but...

"Then what happened?" Piotr goaded.

Babcia sighed.

"The Moon and the Sun had their first argument. Sitting side by side in the sky, the Moon noticed what was wrong before the Sun did. She realised she was being outshone. The

Sun ignored her often, trying to dry up more and more of the sea, thereby killing the silver fish-people, and so the Moon tried to send more water, which drowned the dragonfly-people, until there were almost none of either people left. One fish-person flopped onto the land and had to learn to breathe in new surroundings. We humans come from that fish, you know. We have to learn to cope with new places, new things..."

Piotr gazed at her with wide, wondering eyes.

"Did they make up?"

She wanted to say she didn't know. There had been no way for Babcia to know. But saying "I don't know" is too uncertain for a bedtime story, and she had to get the truth into her grandson in a gentle way, somehow. Life is not always chocolates and roses.

"The Sun left the Moon," she admitted. "But I think you'd guessed that already. Since then, they've always visited the world separately, to see how we are living, because we are their distant grandchildren. They can't forgive each other for trying to destroy each other's children, but this is only because they loved their children very much."

She reached out and combed her fingers through Piotr's hair, enjoying the cosy silence. He had fallen asleep before she got to the end.

Jewel of the Sea

Julie Reeser

She hadn't ever had a true and proper name. The band of outlaws who'd raised her had simply yelled, "Girl!", whenever they needed her to fetch or haul. She'd had a mother, though. A tiny bit of a woman with a voice like thunder and quick hands like startled deer.

One night, her mother told her a tale of whales. She'd insisted they were angels fallen from heaven, so full of grief they wandered the oceans keening. The girl hadn't laughed at that. Looking around their poor hovel, she could believe in angels made of sadness.

When her mother died and her own sorrows piled up beyond what she could bear, she left on the back of her pet reindeer, Bac. A nameless girl would not be missed, and so she didn't bother saying goodbye. Bac was a shaggy beast with a beard of white and hooves like hungry mouths, eating the journey in great gulps. She put her head low against his musky neck and whispered to him her wish to see the whales. He knew just where to go.

Raised by outlaws, her pistol rode on her left hip, her knife on the right. She was ready for trouble, as that was all she'd known in her short life. Soon, the smell of the ocean licked at her hair and her gut tightened with more than hunger. The shimmer of the sea stretched into forever as if the sky looked into a mirror.

Bac sensed her fear and pulled up at the edge of the great harbor. *It isn't too late to go back,* he said with his rough kisses and night-sky eyes. His gray-flecked fur reminded her of the cold-swept plains and snow-covered mountains of home. She gently kissed his antlers farewell, and he lovingly nibbled her braids goodbye.

The sounds of water and wood greeted her and got into her bones. Ships larger than the whole outlaw camp hid the horizon from view. She walked the dock, dodging barefoot men and lean dogs, until she found a ship taller than them all.

She approached the Captain who was built like a tree, his trunk gnarled and his hair like wind-tossed leaves. He stood with one foot planted on the gangway and the other cocked against the polished wood of the quarterdeck.

"What can you do other than gape at the sea?" asked the Captain. In answer, she drew on her luck and shot his parrot clean off his shoulder. The bird, now missing a few feathers, glared at her from the safety of the bowsprit. Blackbeard, for it was he, laughed so hard he swallowed his tobacco.

"Yer hired!" he shouted.

As she stomped up the gangway, he asked her name. She bared her teeth and showed him her knife. He spit off the deck, neatly avoiding his beard, and named her Thorn.

"Ye wave that stick around like ye mean to slice up the world and serve it for dinner."

He had it a'right. She wanted to plunge her knife into the world up to the hilt and then swallow the carcass. She wanted to consume every sight and taste all the delights. There wasn't anything to be done unless it was with both hands and all her might, so she signed her new name to the contract of the *Queen Anne's Revenge* and joined the crew.

When the sails cracked open in the wind the next morning, she jumped for joy. The sound made her insides quiver, and the rocking of the deck made her legs wiggle like she'd danced all night. The men swarmed around her like a kicked ant hill. She followed one squat and grimy pirate to a tangle of hemp as big around as her arm. He grabbed it and pulled hard. She took the bitter end and curled it like a sleeping snake on the deck. It was coarse and smelled like Bac, her reindeer and friend. She was struck with a sudden homesickness, but the work soon made her sweaty, and she forgot to be sad.

The squat pirate was the *Anne's* shanty-man, Jack. It was his duty to lead the pirates in song so their work would have rhythm and be less hard. After their morning chores were completed, he took her to the bilge hold and taught her songs while they pumped out the filthy water.

"Who's that knocking at my door?
Said the fair maiden.
It's only me from over the sea,
Says Barnacle Bill the sailor.
My and my crew have come for a..."

"Oh!" said Jack. He stopped singing as if an adder had bitten his tongue, and his face turned three shades of pink and two types of purple. "I need to be teaching ye a diff'rent sort of ditty. Ye be too young fer that particular song."

He cleared his throat, and Thorn waited. They stopped turning the windlass.

"Are you feeling well?" she asked.

"I be fine. I jess be forgettin' yer tender age and all. How 'bout this one, then?" He pushed forward on the windlass's arm and began to sing again.

"I dreamed my love came in my sleep,
Lowlands, Lowlands, away, my John.
His eyes were wet as he did weep,
My Lowlands, away!
I shall never kiss you again, he said,
Lowlands, lowlands, away, my John.
For I am drowned in the Lowland seas.
My Lowlands, away!
No other man shall think me fair,
Lowlands, Lowlands, away, my John.
My love lies drowned in the windy Lowlands,
My Lowlands, away!"

They finished the song as the last of the water sloshed into the ocean, and Thorn wiped a tear from her cheek.

Jack nodded at her soberly. "Aye, it be worthy of that. A sad one. Let's wash up and get grub."

The bilge wasn't as brown and smelly as it would be once they'd been at sea for days, but the bucket of sea water splashing over Thorn's hands and boots was a relief. She wasn't cleanly or godly, but she didn't want her food to taste like rot.

Thorn cast a critical eye over the lads. She'd been ready to fight any pirate who thought she only belonged in the galley, but Blackbeard had sailed with Calico Jack, and he'd fought and pirated with Mary Read and Anne Bonny, so he and his crew knew a lass would fight and heave as well as they could.

Every muscle and tendon of the crews' sun-drenched skin showed. Their clothes were faded but there was care in the mending. Some of them were missing teeth or fingers, but all wore a gold hoop earring. She fiddled with her own bare lobes and turned to the shanty-man, Jack.

"How do I get one of those?" she asked, sticking out her sharp chin at the gold circlet in his ear.

He gripped the drop of yellow. "Ye be earning it or stealing it. When ye get one, surgeon'll fix ye right up proper-like. Till then, ye best be knowing, we be dropping ye over the side."

"Over the side? Of the ship?" Her heart beat faster.

"Only if ye die," he shrugged. "It ain't so bad. Yer dead, anyhow. Nothing but salt and fishes!" He and a few of the lads laughed at that.

Thorn thought on this for a moment and then jumped to her next question. "Have you ever seen a whale?"

The men got quiet, but Jack answered her. "Aye, a few of us seen the big ones. Robert, there." He pointed with his knife; a piece of meat still speared on it. "He used to sail on a whaler. He can tell ye all about it."

Robert wore an eye patch, and his other eye was stuck in a permanent squint. He kept his head tilted to the left side, as if listening to someone telling him a secret.

"Aye, lass. I seen many a whale in my time."

"Is that how you lost your eye?" she asked.

The pirates leaned forward in anticipation.

"This?" Robert asked and pointed at the patch with his own knife. "Wanna see it?"

Thorn made herself ready by clenching her jaw and putting both hands on the worn wooden table. "Yes." She wouldn't fail this first challenge of her mettle.

Robert slid his finger under the patch and pulled. Thorn gasped, and all the pirates laughed heartily.

"Why, there's nothing wrong with it at all!" she exclaimed.

Between laughter and bites of dinner, he explained. "Nah, it's just as blue as the other. I cover it in case I need to shoot in the below-decks."

"Oh, I see," Thorn said and then realized her joke. She joined in the laughter with the others. She'd passed her first test with flying colors.

The question about whales was forgotten, but Thorn remembered later at pipe-down when she fell into her hammock exhausted. She understood now why all the men looked like they were put together with rope and burnt wax. Every part of her hurt and burned from the work of sailing. Before she drifted into a sleep rocked by swells and troughs, she vowed to go to Robert and ask him more about the whales— the angels of sorrow.

The bosun's whistle and pirates shouting woke her. A battle! She knew enough to lash up and stow her hammock to protect the crew from shot. Her hands were steady, but her heart stuttered like a fish on land. She climbed past the galley and up to the gun deck. The shanty-man was nowhere to be found, so she climbed once more and emerged onto a roaring scene of war.

Pirates dotted the rigging while others heaved and hauled to bring the ship around. There were no lanterns lit. They were sailing hard and fast through the dark like a ghost. Running toward the quarterdeck, her boot caught on the coaming. She fell hard enough to rattle the teeth in her head. Before she could get to her knees, the ship lurched as it was struck, and she tumbled into the ocean.

Blind and cold and thrashing fear.

Thorn was grateful her pirate garb lacked skirts. Bubbles surrounded her, and the ocean was as dark as dirt. The sound of the cannons and battle echoed dully in the murk. She thought she was treading water, but it wasn't true; she was sinking. She kicked off her boots before they could pull her down further. Her bare feet sawed and her arms chopped, and finally her head broke the surface. She sucked at the air in great gulps. Clearing her vision with a shake, she saw how far she had drifted. No one would see her during the fight, and by the time it was over, she'd be too far away to get their attention.

The battle continued with flares from the cannons like dying stars streaking the night sky. A fire broke out on the enemy ship, and a white flag was hoisted. The distant cheers of the *Anne's* crew sounded like wind in the trees back home. Her tears mingled with the ocean waves. There would be a flutter and flurry of panic when they noticed she was gone, but there was nothing to be done. She'd never earned her earring, and she'd been given to the sea just as the shanty-man warned.

Thorn tried to yell to the *Anne*, but every time she opened her mouth, a wave splashed in, and she sputtered and choked. The clouds had drifted as much as she had, and the sky was now an endless velvet cloth pierced with stars. The waves tossed her up and down as if she were a miniature pirate ship. She was getting cold. As she watched, an orange streak dove from one corner of the sky to the other. A wish-maker.

I wish to be rescued so I might meet an angel of sorrow and see the whole of the world, she thought.

Her wish was layered; one had to be clever and grab at life with both hands. "It isn't cheating," she whispered to the stars.

She drowsed and contemplated the cold killing her. Her reindeer had told her stories of the ice and frost of his northern homeland. He said dying from cold was as pleasant as falling asleep. She disagreed.

When she tried to swim, her foot brushed something firm. She yelped in fear and lifted her knees which caused her head to slip underwater. There was a strange light below her, and she dove to see it better.

Whales!

Each was as long as the *Queen Anne* and speckled over with constellations. They called to one another in deep, moaning laments making her bones rumble and her skin tingle. The pod circled what appeared to be a sapphire star, pulsing blue. As she tried to swim closer, her brain screamed for air. Giving up, she kicked her way to the surface.

After taking three rapid deep breaths, she gulped as much night air as she could, and dove once more. The blue light was closer now, and she thought it might be an octopus. It was writhing and shifting shape too rapidly for her to get a clear look.

The whales rose near the surface. They breached and blew spray and sound into the cold. Thorn hooted with joy. She could believe they were angels with their grace and beauty, but they were too vast and alive and alien to be sad. Her mother had been wrong. The whales were joy!

She sang to them with her little voice, and then laughed at herself for being silly. The blue octopus was only a few feet below her now. She sank to examine it.

It continued to cavort and gambol, seemingly oblivious of having an audience. Thorn didn't hesitate but put out her hand toward a tentacle the color of a September sky. It didn't retreat but wrapped the flowing appendage softly around her wrist. They hung suspended in the abyss of the ocean, touching and connected, while the bulk of the whale pod sang around them.

A whale brushed her foot. She turned, and the octopus slid away from her touch. The whale sang a melody, high in pitch, and rolled under Thorn; a reflection of the night sky in white splotches and barnacles. The whale floated upward with her nestled in the furrow of its dorsal ridges. It had two blow-holes, and she screamed with excitement as the whale blew air and salt spray several feet above her. The body underneath her bunched like a fist, and then they shot forward. The water rushed past so quickly, Thorn was afraid she'd fall off.

She gripped the hand-sized barnacles strewn across the whale's skin and braced her bare feet. The barnacles felt like thick eggshells, soft and sandy to her waterlogged hands. The whale breached and kept going up, up, up into the air. Thorn howled with fear and delight. The concussion of the landing knocked her into the water. A barnacle fragmented in her clenched hand. It was only a moment before the whale lifted her once more. She gasped for air and yelled, "Again"!

The whale cackled at her in creaks and whistles. She warbled and cooed in return. It started toward the ships, and she relaxed. It was returning her to the pirates. Returning her home. Her hand still gripped the barnacle's shattered body. She opened her fist, expecting to find blood, but instead found a lump of glittering gold.

She couldn't wait to show Jack! She had earned her earring.

Mama and the Witch

Emily Martha Sorensen

I shall never forget the day Mama snubbed the witch.

It was on Dirasnaide, the last day of the year. Mama wore her best hat and dress, reminding everybody we met that this great day was her birthday. Never mind it was my birthday too—never mind that I wore threadbare hand-me-downs and had no hat at all.

I hugged the back of our procession, as I always did. Being the youngest, I was frequently forgotten or pounded on. Mama spoiled Nadrainli, the oldest, because they'd intended her birth. Papa bragged incessantly about all of his five sons. But I'd been a surprise, four years after Naomi, the final daughter.

"That's right," Mama bragged to the grocer. "It's been thirty-five years since I chased the last witch away. Thirty-five years! On my seventh birthday it was, yet I was smart enough back then to know to rid the town of witches!"

I stared at the shop window glumly. Reuben and Lee were already inside, fighting over the last piece of penny candy in a display. In a minute, Papa would roar in there and give both of them a wallop for their bad behavior.

Papa never walloped me. Papa never noticed me. I'd also never had a penny to spend on candy.

"That's right," Mama went on, preening. "Seventh daughter of a seventh daughter I was, a real plum for any witch to take. But did I go? Oh, no! Stood my ground and spat at her, didn't I? Proved I wouldn't take her nonsense! Proved there was no curse upon me to become one of those things!"

Sometimes I thought there was a curse upon me.

Or rather, I was the curse.

Mama and Papa should have stopped with eleven, I thought glumly. I glanced at my sister Naomi, patting her hair in the shop window. She looked so much like Mama, so prim. *Or, better yet, ten.*

A sneering voice said from behind us, "There weren't no chance yeh was ever goin' to be one of us 'things.'"

Startled, I spun around. Mama did, too. Her face went pale with horror.

"*Witch!*" she cried, pointing.

A hideous old woman wearing a threadbare traveling cape shrugged. "As yeh say."

Mama's face turned bright red. "You've come to try to convert me to your wicked ways again! Admit it!"

The witch sneered. "Yeh can call my ways wicked if yeh want, but yeh ain't got magic, and there's no point in pretendin' yeh do. Yeh ain't a seventh daughter of a seventh daughter. Yer a seventh daughter of an *eighth.*" The witch sniffed. "Now, *her . . .*"

The witch pointed a bony claw towards us. It took me a moment to realize, in horror, that she was pointing at me.

"Annie?" Mama asked, her voice hoarse.

"Didn't it never occur to yeh?" The witch cackled. "Yeh got seven daughters here, same as yer ma. Can't yeh count?"

I stood ramrod still, my heart pounding. What did she mean? Did she mean me? How could that be? Nobody even noticed me!

"Ain't yeh never noticed it?" The witch cackled. "The child goes invisible! How could yeh not realize a thing like that?"

I gasped and took a step backward.

Mama's face was ashen. She said nothing.

The witch laughed. "Blind, alla yeh! Fools! Idiots!"

"Pl-please, stop it!" I gasped. "I'm not a witch! I can't be! Mama —"

Mama's face flooded with crimson. "You will not insult me any longer. Leave, before I —"

"Insult yeh?" the witch jeered. "I ain't half-done insultin' yeh! Look! Yer seventh daughter's invisible right now!"

All heads whipped around, searching for me. I cowered in fear. Wandering eyes searched through me, not seeing me. I breathed a sigh of relief.

And then I realized what it meant. What it had always meant.

I really was a witch.

"Annie?" Ma called, sounding frightened. "Annie?"

"Annie?" Pa roared. "If you're a witch, I'll wallop the magic right outta ya!"

"Annie!" Lee shouted.

"Annie!" Reuben yelled.

"Annie!" Naomi hollered.

"Annie!" Nadrainli cried.

I watched them all silently, realizing for the first time that I didn't have to be a curse to them all anymore. I could be free.

If only I had somewhere to go.

And then I saw the witch's eyes watching me.

She knew where I was even though no one could see me. She was standing right there, waiting for me. She had . . . she had *come* here for me.

Nobody had ever wanted me before.

I walked over to her and silently slipped my hand in hers.

The witch's eyes glinted. "Good choice," she whispered. "Happy seventh birthday. Don't worry, I ain't nearly as wicked as I look."

"I know," I whispered back. "I know what wicked looks like, and it's not you. It's clean and pretty, and it wallops children."

The witch's eyes darkened at first, but then they glinted. She became invisible too, and we walked out of town together.

I shall never forget the day Mama snubbed the witch.

It was the day I started my life.

Thoughtful Young

Malevolent Mrs. Mosely

Rucha Dixit

A gust of wind blew wisps of her hair around as Kim opened the window in her room. She shut her eyes for a moment to feel the cool breeze against her skin.

Surprised to see light coming from the old house next door, she wondered, would there be a family with children, a dog even. The house had been unoccupied for years. Curiosity filled her.

A dark silhouette appeared in the first-floor window of the house opposite hers.

Who's that? Kim thought.

She squinted to look carefully but the figure quickly disappeared.

A few days later, Kim was at her desk near the window, busy with her math assignment. She grimaced at the books and glanced out the window to take a break from the mind-numbing task at hand. A fleeting figure again crossing the window caught her attention. Kim sat up alert and leaned in towards the window, her skin prickling with inquisitiveness for she had seen no one at the house since the first night. Soon she was digging into her closet to retrieve a pair of binoculars. Her uncle had bought them for her when she expressed a passing interest in birds. Now they would help to explore the enigma.

Kim found herself staring into the wrinkly face of an old woman grinning at her from the window. The sight of the near toothless jaw, the thick, round glasses perched on the bridge of a huge, crooked nose caused the binoculars to slip from Kim's clammy hands. Instead of picking them up, she ducked and hid below the window, her heart hammering her ribcage. She knew the woman had seen her and when she finally dared to peek, the window was dark.

That night Kim slept with the window shut tightly and the little brass lock firmly in place behind the pulled curtains.

On Sunday morning, Kim woke to muffled voices downstairs. She peered at the bedside clock with heavy eyes.

Who could that be? And at quarter to 9!

Kim lived only with her Mum, and they usually didn't have visitors especially at that hour. She grabbed her house-robe and hurriedly walked downstairs into the living room.

"Good morning, dear," said a petite old woman with a hunched back.

Kim recognized the face she had seen through her binoculars.

"Mum," she called trying to fight the panic in her mind.

"Morning, darling," Mum said walking out of the kitchen with two cups of tea and a plate of biscuits on a tray. She put the tray down on the coffee table. "This is Mrs. Mosely? She's our new neighbor." Mum turned to the old woman. "Mrs. Mosely, this is my daughter, Kim."

"Hello, Kim."

Kim mumbled back, "Hello."

"What a lovely name! And she's just as lovely," Mrs. Mosely told Mum before sipping her tea.

"Thank you." Mum smiled.

"Thank you, my dear, for the marvellous cuppa."

"You're very welcome. And please, take your time with the lawn mower."

"That's very kind of you. Actually, it would be handy if I could also borrow the hedge trimmer," said Mrs. Mosely.

"Of course. Not a problem. Kim will bring it along."

What? No!! Kim retorted mentally.

Mrs. Mosely walked out of the house, dragging the lawn mower. And Kim dragged herself along with the hedge trimmer at a distance.

"Can I put it down here?" Kim asked, standing in front of the garage of Mrs. Mosely's house, keen to leave.

"It would be very kind if you can place it inside the garage, my dear. These old bones can crack at the slightest weight, you know."

Kim shifted uncomfortably but didn't want to risk looking rude. She picked up the hedge trimmer and took a few unsure steps into the garage before placing it hurriedly on the shelf. In an instant, the garage door slammed shut behind her.

"Now let's get down to business," hissed the old woman.

Kim's heart vaulted inside her chest.

"Wh-what do you want?"

"Oh dear, oh dear," said Mrs. Mosely moving closer to Kim. "Look at the colour in your cheeks and that gorgeous, gorgeous smooth skin. And the silky hair." Her hand came up to stroke Kim's hair; Kim smelt her rotten breath and squirmed. "I would give anything to look young again. Like you. And I will," she said. "You will give it all to me... *I will have your youth!*"

"W-who are you?" Kim stammered, her throat packed with sawdust. Inside her was a tempestuous ocean of nerves.

"Only a *Witch*, my dear," Mrs. Mosely said. "Only a witch can make such a ridiculous demand."

She opened a door at the back of the garage. A sickly white and gray antique cupboard stood like an obscene gravestone next to a huge oak tree shamelessly breaking through the roof, gradually revealed in the reluctant light.

"The only way," continued the old woman, "to be young again is simple. One simply has to swap ages with a young girl just like you!"

Kim's stomach churned, but she pressed on. "You can't do that. Mum will come looking for me any minute."

Mrs. Mosely threw her head back and let out a fit of laughter like a screeching seagull. "I love the innocence...or rather the foolishness! Do you really think I'm that stupid?" Her ugly face contorted obnoxiously as she spoke. "It's not really difficult to keep Mums busy, is it? One tiny little spell, and her sister called as soon as you left. Now that'll give us some time, won't it my dearie? It won't take long, you see. We shall be done in a bit, after which you shall look like a crumply old hag, and I will walk out looking like a pretty young woman. Who and what will poor Mum look for *then*?"

Kim gulped nervously. Mrs. Mosely opened the cupboard and Kim's jaw dropped. Small stoppered vials, some clear, some dark and heavy lined the shallow shelves. Brushing aside the gauzy mass of spider webs the old witch reached in and grabbed a tiny glass ampoule filled with a sparkly green liquid in it that swished and swirled inside the bottle as if both alive and angry.

"Over here," said Mrs. Mosely, snapping her fingers.

In a jiffy, Kim found herself in front of the cupboard. She looked around in disbelief.

"The ASP," Mrs. Mosely bragged, holding out the glass ampoule.

"ASP?!" Kim asked, half-dizzy due to the sequence of events unfolding before her.

"You dim-witted kids these days. It's the Age Swap Potion–ASP, a result of my sheer genius. It took me over a decade's labour to come up with this." The old woman parted her lips in an arrogant grin looking at the bottle with admiration. She swaggered to Kim. "I can't wait any more. I am so dreadfully tired of looking like this at eighty-one. Soon I will drink it and cast a spell and any living thing that drinks it after; which is you..." She poked Kim, "...swaps ages with me."

Holding the bottle of sizzling ASP to her lips, Mrs. Mosely screamed, "TRANSALATO SENECTIUS!" and poured a spoonful of it into her mouth. Kim watched in horror.

"Now take this and gulp it down to complete the age swap." Mrs. Mosely held out the bottle of ASP. "Ah-ah," she said holding it back for a moment. "Dare not drop it or try to run. If you do, I shall pin you down with a spell and force it into your mouth. So be a good girl and don't make me break any of those beautiful teeth." She handed the bottle to Kim.

Kim held the bottle with sweaty, shaky hands and took a few uncertain steps backwards. Those few seconds stretched themselves like eternity.

"Come on then, you clumsy little wretch. I don't have all day."

Startled, Kim stumbled over the roots of the oak behind her and broke the fall with one of her hands, sitting down with a soft thud. She could feel the dense, voluminous, lateral roots of the oak beneath the palm of her hand. Something clicked in Kim's head. Without further ado, she opened the bottle and poured the green fluid into the roots of the oak tree. The fluid flowed into the roots with a hissing sound and instantly disappeared into the gnarled wood.

"Nooooooooooooooooo!" screamed the old woman.

Her body twisted and knotted into a three-hundred-and-something-year-old heap.

Ever seen a fossil? She was no different.

The oak's trunk shrank and shrank until it was about a third its original girth. After all it was now a youthful eighty-one!

Thoughtful Young

Collector of Broken Dreams

Jessica Artemisia Mathieu

In the town *Shush*, a town hidden between places, lives the Collector of Broken Dreams. Her name is Elda, and each night, she trudges past homes, collecting the dreams heaped in broken pieces on doorsteps and under windowsills.

She picks them up and places them carefully in her wooden handcart. No one has seen Elda's face in many lifetimes. No one knows if anyone has ever seen Elda's face. And no one cares. In fact, no one ever thinks about Elda, and this is how she wants it. That's why she took the post as Collector of Broken Dreams. The less people are reminded of her existence, the better.

So every night, Elda walks the ancient stone streets, and just before the sun is ready to break triumphantly into the sky, she brings her overflowing cart to the center of the city where the Pool waits. Here, Elda drops in the mostly darkened pieces of dreams. What had remained of their light had died sometime in the night.

The Pool is special, you see. It is the fountain of energy from which the town draws life.

This is Elda's life. For her it is all very normal. Each night the same, almost always.

On one such night Elda found a child's dream broken in the street beneath a window. A little girl sat in the window above it, crying softly, so that only Elda's membrane ears, sensitive to the slightest changes in vibration in the air around her, could hear.

"Tch, little one," thought Elda with tenderness in her heart. She picked up the child's broken dream and gingerly tucked it into her cloak. The pieces of the child's dream still glowed with hope, even as the little girl cried inconsolably in the room above the street. She never saw Elda, and she never would. That's the way Elda likes it. As Elda sees it, it doesn't matter who sews the dreams back together. It only matters for those rare dreams that cling to life, that never died.

Just as the sun began to whisper to the sky of her return, Elda deposited the broken dreams in the Pool. She reached a hand beneath her cloak to the little girls dream, she smiled when she felt that it still lived and headed home. On the way, she stopped by the Field of Unicorns and picked through the trash there. Unicorns love to brush their manes and tails, and even though they rarely shed, because they have never met Time, sometimes a strand will break. Elda uses these rare strands to mend broken dreams.

Back home in her hut nestled in the mangroves that edged the lily ponds, Elda set to work on the child's dream. The dream hummed with hope. Each stitch of unicorn thread strengthened the flickering life.

Elda sat and hummed with the dream as she worked, and by nightfall, the child's dream was sewn back together. Pleased, Elda sat back in her chair with a smile and wiped a sinewy arm across her damp brow. It is hard, exacting work, to build the flickering hope in the broken dream. As she made her even, tiny stitches, she hummed in chorus with the dream to the Great One, asking for grace and to borrow the Light. The hard part was keeping her heart empty in order to receive it, so she might pour it through her hands into her work. This time, she was granted success.

Elda stood up, her gnarled joints creaking (she had met Time long ago, and in fact, they were good friends), and tucked the dream into her vest. She shrugged on her cloak, fed what could easily be called a cat, and took up the handles of her handcart.

She spent the whole night collecting and as the sun began kissing the sky to the east, Elda walked hesitantly to the home of the child.

Not all people with broken dreams want the dream back, she knew. But she could tell the dream wanted to return, so maybe there was hope. Elda placed the dream on the doorstep and rang the bell. Then she scuttled off to a nearby corner to hide behind some vines overflowing from a private garden. Most people don't notice Elda, anyway, even if they are looking right at her, but Elda didn't want to take any chances.

The light on the stoop lit up and the door opened a crack.

"Hello?" came a small girl's voice. "Is someone out there?" A head peaked out and looked around, then, looking down, she saw the glowing dream on her doorstep. The small figure gasped and picked up the dream, holding it close. She squeezed it so hard Elda thought it might break again, but it didn't. It hummed with love. Its own light seemed to return the child's embrace.

From that night on, Elda heard singing coming from the child's bedroom, and she could see the small figure silhouetted in the bright room. Over the years, the child grew, but not very much, and her posture became gnarled, like Elda's joints, but the girl continued to sing and sing, and her voice was so beautiful that people came to hear. One night, Elda saw a poster at the local theatre proclaiming a night of heavenly beauty, and on it was a picture of a girl who hadn't grown like the other girls, straight and tall, but rather, she had grown up twisted and bent.

Elda was happy. That morning, after she had returned the broken dreams to be recycled in the Pool, she sat on the little porch of her hut on the edge of the lily pond. As the sun unfolded its pink, red, and orange dance across the morning sky, Elda listened to the chorus of croaks and trills and caws and warbles as her neighbors sang about their lives in the lily pond. She sang quietly to herself in a heavenly voice no one could hear which belonged neither in the lily pond, nor on the stage.

Thoughtful Young

The Boy Who Said Boo

J.C.G. Goetz

Bartholomew B. Bartholomew was the boy who said boo. The very first word he ever said, before momma, or poppa, or gimmee, was "boo."

When Bart was very little, his father would play "peekaboo" with his son. To Bart, "boo" meant, "I am very happy to see you, and am most excited about spending some time with you."

"Boo" was just about the best word ever to Bart, even after he learned hundreds and thousands more. Bart would say "boo" whenever he could, particularly when he met someone new.

At first, the people in Bart's village smiled and laughed when he said, "Boo!"

Some of the villagers would say, "Look at that boy who said, 'Boo!' Isn't that the most precious thing?"

One of the villagers said, "He must think he's a ghost."

"He seems like a friendly ghost," another villager said.

Tormentilla Tillotson sneered when she saw the villagers fawn over Bartholomew. She said, "I think he is a right proper *monster!*"

The villagers all laughed, but the name stuck. Whenever Bart said, "Boo!" they called him a little monster.

At first Bart laughed when they called him a monster, for he didn't really know what a monster was. Then he went into his father's library and found a big book and looked up the word, monster. The book had pictures of monsters, and they were all ugly and frightening.

He ran to the bathroom and looked in the mirror. He said, "I am not a monster. I'm not huge and strange and ugly. I don't have horns or tusks or three eyes. I'm not green or purple or gray."

The next time Bart went to town, when someone called him a monster, he said, "I am not a monster. I don't have horns or tusks!"

Tormentilla sneered again and said, "That's just because you are little. When you grow up, you will have horns on the top of your head and shaggy fur all over your back."

Bart ran home and cried. He touched the top of his head, and he thought he felt the nubs of horns just starting to poke through the top of his scalp, under his hair. He pulled up the back of his shirt and looked in the mirror: one hair grew from his back.

When he went to town, the people called him a monster and pointed out the hideous defects that were just beginning to grow. Soon he had to hide behind hedges because people would throw stones or set their dogs after him.

Each time he looked in the mirror, he could see more of the defects that the villagers saw in him. Well, he *couldn't see* them exactly, but he knew they were there, just below the surface of his skin. His teeth were getting longer and sharper; he was sure of it.

One night, Bart had a bad dream. He was playing peekaboo with his father, and when he said, "Boo!" his father's face froze in horror. His father called him a monster. Bart grew so large that he towered over his father and gobbled him up in one bite. Bart heard the villagers yelling and their dogs barking, so he ran away and hid.

When Bart woke up, he was huddled under a bush, far away from his house. He had no place to go. The villagers hated him, and he didn't want to turn into a monster and eat his father, who had always been so good to him.

Bart started to cry but knew that wouldn't do a bit of good. No one would come to help him, because he was such a monster. He had to run away into the wilderness.

He didn't have a home, so he had to sleep on the ground or in a tree. No one would feed him, so he had to find his own food. He could never find enough berries to eat, so he began to eat grass and leaves to sate his hunger. He even hunted field mice and nestlings and ate them raw.

Despite his lack of food, Bart grew larger. Soon enough, all the claims of the villagers came true. *If everyone calls you a monster, it often comes true, if you let it.* He grew horns like a deer and tusks like a boar. One ear moved down and the other moved up. His right eye looked left, and his left eye looked right. His back hunched over, and prickly black hair grew out of his thick red skin. He grew so large and strong that he could pull a tree out by its roots.

People of the village began to tell stories about the troll in the woods, and everyone forgot that Bartholomew B. Bartholomew had ever existed.

Whenever a child or pet went missing, the troll was blamed. Eventually, the villagers decided to burn the forest down to get rid of the monster.

The villagers formed a line with their torches and set the woods on fire. By the time the fire reached Bart, it raged through the tops of the trees, and he had to run on all four limbs, like a bear, to get away. He ran to some rocky hills where he found a cave to hide in.

He escaped the fire, but some of the villagers were not so lucky. Tormentilla Tillotson was caught by the fire and flared up like fat that had dripped into a barbecue grill.

Bart watched the fire from the mouth of the cave. He felt sorry for the villagers that died in the fire, because he didn't know they were trying to kill him. The fire was dying down when he heard a small, high voice from the back of the cave.

"Hello there," she said. "I'm Filomena."

Bart reacted before he could stop. "Boo!" he said.

Something very wonderful happened. Filomena laughed. She didn't call him a monster. The late afternoon sun shone deep into the cave. Filomena was nearly as tall as Bart, but one leg was much longer than the other, and her shoe on the short leg had a very high heel. The arm on the side of her long leg was very short, and the arm on the side of her short leg was very long. Her neck was long on one side and short on the other, so her head was cocked to the side, one ear touching her shoulder, and the other on the "top" of her head. She looked like she was made of thick, crinkly white paper, drawn on with black ink, but her eyes and smile were warm.

"We've been wondering when you would come here," said Filomena.

"You have?" asked Bart. "Who are you, and how did you know about me?"

"I'm Filomena F. Filomena, and I live in a city that is at the other end of this cave. We'd like you to live with us. We know about you because we know a little bit about everything. I think you'd like living with us."

"It's very nice of you to ask, but the people of the village cast me away because I'm a monster. I don't think the people of your city would care for me."

"I was cast away by my village too, because I'm a freak. My city is full of monsters and freaks."

Bart wanted nothing more than to be with other people. He wanted someone to say "boo" and mean, "I am very happy to see you and am most excited about spending some time with you." He couldn't imagine what a city of monsters and freaks would be like. It might be very nice, but he was afraid too.

"It might be very nice, but I'm afraid," he admitted.

Filomena startled: her eyes got big and she covered her mouth with her hand. "A big monster like you?"

"Sometimes people threw rocks at me, and they even hurt when they didn't hit me."

"We don't throw rocks," said Filomena. "We really are excited about spending time with you. I'm very happy to have met you."

There was a space in Bart that had been empty ever since he left his home. Right now, that space was filling with his tears, but it didn't feel that bad to cry at all. Sometimes crying leaves you empty, and other times it fills you up. This was one of the good, filling-up times.

"Yes, I'd like to go to your city with you. I'm very happy to have met you, and I am really excited about spending time with you." Bart shrugged. "Boo."

Filomena laughed and said, "Boo!" She led Bart through the cave. At the other end, the cave opened onto the side of a mountain. Golden sunlight hit them, and the city shone in the valley below. It was a place of crystal spires, with silver roads that wound through the air, linking the spires. Almost every other block had a playground or park.

"I've never seen anything like this," said Bart. "Not even in books!"

Filomena patted his hand. "Freaks and monsters make the best things."

Bart looked down at her hand on his. His skin wasn't red and hairy! She didn't look like she was made of paper. She was a beautiful woman (for all people are beautiful, if you know how to look at them), and he was a handsome young man.

"Boo!" said Bartholomew.

"Likewise," said Filomena.

Thoughtful Young

Breaking the Brownie Code

Anthea Sharp

It wasn't a simple thing, cleaning a cottage in a wink while the humans slumbered. And to be honest, Feeyah MacGuire was not the most accomplished of brownies—as her boss, Biddy Porter, was even now pointing out.

"There's enough dust under that bed to fill a frying pan," Biddy said, in her most disappointed voice. "The kettle isn't nearly polished enough, and I found a large spot of jam on the countertop." She shook her head in a now familiar fashion. "Feeyah, you're a disgrace to the profession."

Feeyah dropped her gaze to the pointed tips of her leather slippers. Shame and a tiny bit of anger mixed hotly in her blood.

"I didn't ask to be born a brownie," she said.

It didn't help matters that she was allergic to dust, and too much scrubbing made the skin of her hands red and itchy. She loathed the fact that she was compelled to rise well before sunup to scrub and sweep and polish and tidy, and her only reward was a sip of milk from a wooden bowl. She usually was the last brownie to finish her chores, and so got the last bit of milk—barely a mouthful. Sometimes less, if the others were greedy.

"Fix your hair and finish up," Biddy said, with a disapproving look at the wisps that had escaped from Feeyah's bun. "I'll be back to check your work, and this cottage had best be neat as a pin. Don't forget to tidy up the child's blocks."

Biddy glanced at the corner where the child slept, a scattering of wooden blocks on the slate floor around his bed.

"Yes'm," Feeyah said.

Truly, what else could she do?

Despite her complete ineptness at cleaning, she had the call in her blood. Oh, she'd tried to ignore the compulsion that woke her from her warm dreams into the cold wee hours of the night, but it was an itch that became a red-hot goad if she did not rise and join the other brownies at their work.

She had considered running away from the clan to seek a different life. Perhaps, once she left the Big Peoples' house, fled from the hidden brownie dwellings and the company of her own kind, she would be free.

But a brownie alone was easy prey for foxes and owls. Without a safe haven to go to, she wouldn't last one night outside by herself. If the animals didn't eat her, there were other, darker folk who would find much sport in tormenting a mild-mannered brownie: the spriggans with their long, pointed nails, the redcap goblins who delighted in mayhem, or even the malicious sprites who led creatures astray to wander forever lost.

Despite her unhappiness, the clan kept her safe.

Feeyah heaved a sigh, then took her broom and ducked under the bed. The dust made her sneeze, but brownie magic kept her from waking the humans who snored above her. More's the pity.

And yet...what if she tried to deliberately rouse the humans?

It was a daring, dreadful thought, but as she swept, the notion would not let her go. She finished her sweeping and magicked away the broom and dustpan. Heart pounding, she poked the loose strands of her plain brown hair back into her bun, then went to the foot of the bed and let herself rise up. Brownies could levitate themselves. How else could they dust the cobwebs from the rafters and reach the difficult corners behind the stove?

She wobbled a bit and grabbed at the bedpost to steady herself in the air. It was one thing to use her magic for cleaning, another altogether to attempt to meddle with mortal folk. Carefully, she landed on the wool blanket beside the wife's feet. The sleeping lumps of the humans rose before her like low hills.

Oh, but this was wicked of her. Brownies were not to be seen by mortal eyes. It was one of the most important points of the Brownie Code. But Feeyah was so bone-weary of her tasks, she was willing to break the code.

If the Big People saw her, what then?

She did not know—but she had heard dire whisperings and half-told tales. But certainly everything would change. It must, for she could not keep scraping along in misery.

Breath fluttering in her lungs, she crept alongside the sleeping wife until she stood beside the pillow. The woman's chest rose up and down in her dreaming, like the surface of the sea, and her face was smoothed of cares. Feeyah lifted her hand, and—

"Feeyah! Hist, away with you!" Biddy materialized beside her, wrapped her stout arms about Feeyah's waist, and pulled her to the floor.

They landed with a bump on the flagstones, and Feeyah pulled out of Biddy's grasp.

"Whatever were you thinking?" Biddy's gaze was hard as ice.

"I just, I wanted..." The words clogged in Feeyah's throat.

"You're perilously close to trouble, young miss," Biddy glanced over to the kitchen. "The kettle is still tarnished. If you don't get back to work, there'll be no milk left for you at all. Is that what you want?"

Feeyah shook her head, tears prickling hotly at the corners of her eyes.

"I'm not fit for the work," she said in a low voice.

"Of course you are." Biddy straightened her apron. "You're a brownie, after all. Now back at it."

She made a shooing motion with her hands, and Feeyah glumly levitated herself up to the kitchen counters. She conjured a scrap of linen and a dab of polish and set to work on the kettle. Half of the metal cleaned up fine, but as Feeyah kept working she ended up smearing soot back over the part she had already polished.

She fetched a new rag, but try as she might, the blasted kettle would not stay clean and unsmudged.

Perhaps she needed a little water from the basin in the sink. She trudged over the counters, not watching her step, and her shoe stuck fast in the spot of jam she'd neglected to scrub. Her rag went flying and down she went, hands before her to break her fall.

A hot flash of pain in her wrist made her cry out, and the sleeping couple mumbled in their dreams. But they didn't wake.

Feeyah sat cross-legged on the counter, wrist cradled in her lap while tears washed her face. Oh, she was most useless, clumsy brownie who had ever lived. Perhaps she *would* slip out at dawn, alone into the wide and terrifying world, and let her fate take her. The clan would be glad enough to be rid of her.

"Why're you crying?" It was a quiet voice, but unmistakably human.

She darted her head up. The child had woken, and was sitting up in his small bed at the far side of the room, looking directly at her. He slipped from between the covers and padded over to the kitchen. A youngling still, his nose came to just above the countertops, and his dark hair stood up in dream-tangled tufts.

"Can you see me, then?" Feeyah hiccupped back her tears and wiped her eyes with the back of her uninjured hand.

"Of course. Seen you lots of times," the boy said in a matter-of-fact tone. "Did you hurt yourself?"

She blinked at him a moment, trying to absorb the fact that the boy had seen her with no measurable consequences whatsoever. So much for her thought of waking his parents. So much for the notion that being seen by humans would change anything.

"Aye," she said after a moment. "Twisted me wrist."

"Stay here," the boy said, his face lighting. "I'll help you."

He darted back to his bed and pulled out a worn stuffed bear with a kerchief fastened about one fuzzy leg. The boy fumbled at the knots, then pulled the linen free and hurried back to where Feeyah sat.

"I'm a good doctor," he said. "Bumble's leg is all better now, so you can use his bandage. We'll make you a sling."

He tied two corners together in a clumsy knot and held it up.

"Come closer," he said.

Feeyah stood, then hesitated. Was this a trap? But the boy's brown eyes were clear and innocent. Swallowing past the lump of fear in her throat, she went to the edge of the counter, then ducked her head and let the boy slip the makeshift sling over her head.

Even though it was a small kerchief, the corners hung down past her knees. She was certain she must look ridiculous.

"Better?" the boy asked.

"Aye."

Her wrist still throbbed, but his kindness warmed her. And she had to admit, her arm felt a touch better inside the support of the cloth.

A flicker of motion caught her eye, and she saw Biddy waving urgently to her from behind the butter churn. The older brownie was scowling, with a look fierce enough to strike moths from the air.

"You'd best be getting back into your bed," Feeyah said to the boy.

Disappointment shadowed his face. "Maybe...maybe when you feel better you could come and play with me?"

"Perhaps I shall." She owed the child a debt of kindness now, and faeries always paid their obligations. "Back to dreaming you go, young lad."

"My name's Ian," he said. "What's yours?"

Biddy shook her head violently, and Feeyah narrowed her eyes. She might be a poor excuse for a brownie, but she was not fool enough to give away her true name.

"You can call me Fee," she said. "Good night."

Biddy lifted her palm and blew an invisible puff of slumberdust at the boy. He yawned, then turned and, without another word, climbed back beneath the covers. In moments his eyes had closed and his chest rose and fell with the even breaths of sleep.

"Feeyah MacGuire!" Biddy stormed out from her hiding place, her voice sharp with wrath. She fetched up before Feeyah, sparks nearly crackling off her small form, and jammed her hands on her hips.

"I didn't mean to—" Feeyah began.

"Just look at you! Speaking with a human, and—worst of all—accepting clothing from him. Oh, you've done more than broken the code, girl, you've shattered it completely."

Feeyah plucked at the sling fastened about her neck, her arguments dissolving at the tip of her tongue. It might not have been meant that way, but the truth of the matter was that a kerchief was, indeed, an item of clothing.

Which meant…

"Am I free, then?" The thought trembled against her heart, exhilarating and alarming.

"The council will have to take it up." Biddy blew an irritated breath from her nostrils. "Now come along. Clearly you can work no more today."

Feeyah cast a last look at the sleeping boy. Gratitude flashed through her, overriding the throbbing pain in her wrist. Then she meekly turned and followed Biddy back to the hidden brownie enclave.

Firelight flickered over the seamed faces of the brownie leaders. The three elders of the council sat in ornately carved wooden chairs before the wide hearth in the common room. Feeyah stood on the flagstones before them, feeling like a fawn before a pack of wolves.

Old Tuck puffed away at his pipe, Eilis knitted on the endless scarf she always had in her lap, and Seamus narrowed his stone-gray eyes at Feeyah. His gaze flicked down to the sling she wore, then back up to her face.

"It cannot be denied," he said in his gravelly voice. "Feeyah MacGuire has accepted a gift of clothing from a human, and is no longer bound to serve in the household."

"What's to be done with her?" Old Tuck asked, blowing a smoke ring to punctuate the question.

Feeyah clenched her uninjured hand, wishing she could ask for mercy. But she was guilty as charged, and to speak now meant her punishment would be even more severe. Fear gripped her in its sharp jaws as she thought of what the consequences of breaking the Brownie Code might be.

"Send her to the Drummond clan," Eilis said. Her needles clacked in time to the words. "If she survives the journey, they'll take her in."

"Feeyah's my wife's cousin's niece," Seamus said. "I can't just expel her and force the lass to make her way in the world."

"She'll be eaten up in a trice." Old Tuck laughed, as if the idea amused him.

Feeyah shivered. So, it was to be the foxes and goblins, after all.

"Oh, stop it." Eilis set her needles down and fixed Old Tuck with a glare. "You're frightening the lass."

"She deserves it, too," Seamus said. "Imagine, letting a human see her."

"The boy said he'd seen me before," Feeyah blurted. "Many times."

Three sets of wise old eyes turned upon her, and she wished the floor would swallow her up.

"Did he now?" There was a mildness in Seamus's voice she knew better than to trust.

"That surprises me not a bit," Eilis said.

"Hmph." Old Tuck took another puff on his pipe. "I suppose what's done cannot be undone. Clearly the boy can hold his tongue."

"Tell me." Seamus leaned forward, his wooden chair creaking. "Did the boy ask anything of you?"

"Yes," Feeyah said, her throat so dry she could scarcely form the words. She paused to swallow.

"Well? Out with it," Old Tuck demanded.

"He asked if I might come play with him, once my wrist healed," she said.

"Ha!" Eilis cackled. "Clever lad, that. You're bound to do so, my girl, do you understand?"

"Aye," Feeyah said.

"That's settled, then," Seamus said. "You'll have to remain with the clan. Now, where's my ale?"

It was a clear dismissal. Feeyah curtsied to the elders. Old Tuck frowned, as though she had gotten off far too lightly, but Eilis gave her a sly wink. Seamus just waved her away as if she were a buzzing gnat. Moving as quietly as her leather shoes would take her, Feeyah left the common room and went back to the dormitory where the unmarried brownie women lived, herself included.

The room was empty, the other women still at their chores, but soon the half-dozen of them would be back, filling the air with their chatter and questions. Questions she hardly knew how to answer.

With a shaky sigh, she sat upon the coarse woolen blanket covering her bed.

"Well, then." Biddy strode into the room and regarded Feeyah. "Seems as though you've come out of this well enough, my girl. Now, let's see to that wrist of yours."

oOo

For seven happy years, Feeyah was playmate and confidante to young Ian as he grew from a sweet boy to a gangly tree of a lad. His parents laughed and shook their heads whenever he played with his "imaginary friend," and Feeyah was very careful to never let them catch a glimpse of her.

She had, at last, gained some wisdom in the brownie ways. She'd gained a husband as well, and two sweet young bairns that filled their home with mischief and laughter.

Still, when the day came that she stood at Ian's bedside and he could no longer see her, sorrow opened a small, permanent hole in the corner of her heart.

Slowly, she pulled a worn kerchief from her pocket and dabbed at her eyes. The linen soaked up her tears, darkening the tiny square of cloth.

Feeyah held it a moment, then with a single shake and muttered word, dispelled the brownie magic she had laid upon it. The kerchief billowed out, once more its original size. Carefully, she laid it on the end of Ian's bed. A full-sized bed it was now, no longer the small truckle he'd used to sleep in.

"Farewell," Feeyah said, in a voice he could not hear. "May many fine adventures await you, my strong and merry lad."

"Hey," he said, snatching the kerchief up. Even though Feeyah stood less than a handspan away, he did not see her. Would never see her again. "Where'd this old thing come from?"

He rubbed at Feeyah's tearstains with his thumb, then shrugged and shoved the kerchief in his pocket. Whistling, he rose and strode from the cottage into the bright sunshine of a summer's morn.

Feeyah watched him go. She swallowed her sorrow—but already something was taking its place. A need, a calling lodged deep in the core of her.

It seemed her reprieve from cleaning was finally at an end.

With a sigh, she turned and pulled his bedcovers straight. Heavy of heart, light of spirit, she conjured up her old broom and began to sweep.

Thoughtful Young

Stopping to Care

Ken Grant

Christina Valenzuela paced quietly, yet confidently as she waited for the contest to begin. She had been selected, of course, as one of the two top eleven-year-olds from her district to compete against other two-person teams from all over the county. She had no doubt her team would win.

She always won.

She was prepared.

She was excited.

She was ready to go.

"Chris."

"It's Christina, Kyle."

Only her grandmother was allowed to call her 'Chris,' and only because she couldn't stop her, and, of course, because her grandmother spoiled her rotten.

Kyle annoyed her. Not because he was Kyle, Christina just hated being part of a team. She was the best, and partners only slowed her down. But there was nothing she could do about it.

"Sorry."

Kyle knew all about Christina's volatile temper. He had tried to be friends for the last couple of years, but he just kept putting his foot in his mouth. The good thing was that Christina was smart and ruthless, so they had a good chance to win.

"You ready, Christina?"

"Yes, Kyle. Now please be quiet."

"Aren't we supposed to work as a team?"

"Yes. Your job is to stay out of my way, and my job is to win this thing."

A loud bell rang out through the valley.

"Competitors begin."

Christina glared at Kyle before checking her wrist for the appropriate coordinates and setting off at a quick pace. Each team member was supplied with a wrist unit that contained the coordinates for the next station. She assumed Kyle was following somewhere behind, but it didn't matter. She was the best and didn't need the help. She reached the first station and placed her hand on the unit, but was rewarded with complete silence.

"What's wrong with this stupid thing?"

"Something wrong, Christina?"

Christina turned and stared daggers at Kyle. Suddenly she understood what was wrong.

"Get over here.

Kyle smiled and sauntered over just slow enough to make Christina fume, and placed his hand on the unit. It activated.

"A group of owls is referred to by this name."

The unit announced the question, then waited for an answer.

"Easy." Christina exclaimed with glee. She knew this one and quickly typed in her answer: PARLAMENT.

"Incorrect answer."

The tone of the station seemed to mock Christina. She usually liked technology, but not right now. "No way. I'm never wrong."

Christina screamed her frustration through clenched teeth.

Kyle peered over her shoulder to see what she had typed. "Are you sure about your spelling there, Christina?"

"I don't spell things wrong."

Christina looked at what she had typed and realized her error. "Oh, parliament."

She typed the word and waited anxiously.

"Answer correct. You can now move to your next station."

"Thanks, Kyle," she mumbled.

"You're welcome."

"You know that spelling makes no sense?"

"Of course."

Christina took off at a trot. She was *not* going to lose. Losing was never an option. Her father had drilled that into her. Being a winner meant you never allowed yourself to let up for one moment.

Christina reached the next station, placed her hand on it for identification, and glared at Kyle to hurry up. Kyle followed Christina's lead, and the next question was announced.

"The number of innings that constitute an official baseball game."

"I know that one," said Kyle, exulting that he had something more to offer the partnership than just spelling.

"Nine."

Kyle entered his answer and threw his hands up in a victory celebration.

"Improper response."

"This thing is crazy. A baseball game is nine innings."

"Do games ever go less than nine innings?"

Kyle looked at Christina and thought for a moment. His eyes grew large, and he slapped his forehead.

"Of course. Sometimes they have to stop the game because of rain. The losing team has to have batted at least five innings. You're amazing, Christina."

"Well, go ahead and type it in."

Kyle typed in the answer and smiled broadly.

"Answer correct. Go to next station."

Christina took off at nearly a run, but then stopped abruptly, Kyle smashed into her back, causing them both to stumble. Kyle was shocked. Christina never stopped for any reason.

"What's going on?" Kyle asked. He looked at a narrow strip of path with a fall-off on either side. "Afraid of heights, Christina?"

"Terrified," she admitted.

Kyle had never imagined Christina could be afraid of anything. He had always thought of her as indestructible. "I'll help you across."

"You will?" she asked in a quavering voice.

"Of course. You can do this, Christina. You can do anything."

Christina stared at the narrow path knowing that it was the only way to reach the next station and that it was the only way that she could win.

Kyle backed onto the path ahead of her, he hands out.

"You won't let me fall. I'm trusting you, Kyle."

"I know."

Christina gripped Kyle's hands and locked her gaze on his eyes. She noticed they were brown, with flecks of green, and took her first step, and then another. She felt Kyle's hands holding tightly to her own and that was enough. It felt oddly good to allow someone else to be strong for a little while, but only for a little while. She wanted so much to be back in control.

"You made it," he said. And looking down, she saw they were once again on the wide path with trees on either side.

"*We* made it," she said without thought.

They quickly moved to the next station, placed their hands on the unit in unison, and waited.

"What three colors are displayed on the flag of the nation of Mexico?"

"Mexico! Why would they expect us to know anything about the flag of Mexico?" Kyle put a fist to his forehead. It was all that he could do to learn about things in his own country. "Why would they want us to know about things in other countries?"

"Everything isn't just about the United States. I'm very proud of my heritage. The colors of the flag of Mexico are green, white, and red." Christina entered the colors and beamed with pride.

"Correct. Move to the next station."

Kyle gave Christina a high five, and they returned the way they had come. This time Christina was a little more confident and simply followed with her hands on his shoulders. The moment that they reached the other side, a cry reached their ears.

"You hear that?" asked Kyle, looking off the main path for the source of the plea.

"I'm sure they're fine, probably couldn't read the coordinates."

"We need to check," said Kyle stepping into the bushes.

"What are you doing?"

Kyle turned toward Christina and stared at her for a moment before responding. "Someone's in trouble. I am going to help."

He started to turn back, but Christina cried out. "I can't win this without you. We'll tell somebody when we get to the end."

He looked at her with a pained expression. He felt sorry for Christina. She'd been taught to win, but no one had taught her to care. "I'm doing this." Kyle spoke with more confidence than he felt. Was it fair to Christina to just make this decision? "It's the right thing," he said and turned back towards the cry. A dozen steps later he knew he had made the right decision.

A girl was sitting, her back against a tree, rubbing her ankle, she was clearly in distress.

"I'm hurt." The girl's large brown eyes drove right through Kyle.

"Let me help," he said. My name's Kyle."

"I'm Andrea."

"What happened?"

"I stepped wrong. I think I sprained my ankle."

"Where's your partner?"

"He left me."

"I won't leave you."

"Thank you."

"My partner, Christina is coming. We can get you out of here and back to a safe place."

An angry looking Christina stepped out of the brush behind him.

"She says her ankle is hurt. We have to help her get back to base and get her ankle tended to."

"But we won't win, Kyle."

"It's not always about winning, Christina. Sometimes it's about doing the right thing. Are you going to help me or not?"

Christina smiled sweetly through clenched teeth and moved to help Kyle lift the injured girl to her feet.

"This is Andrea," Kyle said.

"I'm Christina," she said curtly

"Thank you so much for helping me," said Andrea. "I wasn't sure if anyone would hear me. I've been calling out for quite a while now. My partner deserted me."

"You can thank Kyle. It was his idea."

Andrea smiled as they set out. An hour later, sweating and dirty, they crossed the finish line with Andrea between them.

"We need help," said Kyle.

Two assistants immediately came forward and took Andrea between them.

"Thank you so much," Andrea called to them as she disappeared from view.

"Congratulations."

Kyle and Christina turned. The chairman with his tailored suit and bold, striped tie stepped in front of them. In his hand were a pair of trophies.

"What," she said, knowing this trophy would never be on her shelf.

"You and Kyle are our winners."

"I don't understand," she said. We didn't finish.

"But you did," he said. The last station was a little different from the others. It involved showing compassion for a person in need. When our board last met, some of our members were concerned that winning at all cost was becoming too much of a focus. We decided to add a wrinkle to the competition. We wanted to see if any of the teams would stop to help someone in need even if it meant losing. Sadly, you and Kyle were the only team that stopped to help."

"She wasn't actually injured, was she?"

"No, but she could have been. You two showed real compassion, and so you are our winners."

Christina looked over at Kyle. She knew who the real champion was. It had been Kyle who had demanded they stop and help. As she looked at Kyle, she liked what she saw, and she gave him a wide, warm smile.

Gremlins in the Attic

Lindsey Morrison Grant

Hannah had just moved to a new neighborhood. She felt sad and alone.

This made Mom sad, too. She wanted her little girl to be happy and to have fun.

"Hannah," she said. "Why don't you go to the park? There were kids there when we drove by. I'm sure they would love to play with you."

"Mom," said Hannah," no one plays with the new kid!"

"Everyone is the 'new kid' sometime, sweetie. Please try," Mom said

"Okay, Mom," the sad little girl said. "I'll go."

"That's my girl! I bet you'll have some new friends before you know it. I can't wait to hear all about it when I get home from work."

When she got to the park, Hannah saw lots of kids having fun. She sat on a rock and turned her back to them. They were playing on the slides and swings, running and jumping, shouting and laughing. They *all* seemed to be having fun, but after a while they all went home.

"All alone again," Hannah said to herself. Just then she heard a voice come from behind her.

"I bet you're wondering why I'm green," the voice said. Hannah turned around and saw a creature who was dressed *just like her!* "My name is Garry. Garry Gremlin."

He was fuzzy and green with big, pointy ears and sharp teeth. "Gremlins only come in one color...green," Garry said. "I came to the park hoping to find a friend, but everyone went home."

"Not everyone," Hannah said. "I'm still here."

"Don't you have a home to go to?" the gremlin asked,

"Yes," said Hannah, "but I get lonely, no one is there to play with me."

175

"What if I go home with you?" he asked. "Then we can play there."

"That would be great!" she said. "I'm Hannah, with two H's, two N's, and two A's. It's the same frontward as backward."

Hannah and Garry had fun in the park. Then they laughed and played all the way home. "Now," Hannah thought, "Garry is not a stranger anymore."

Hannah and Garry played games and colored in coloring books. When Cartoon Castle was over, Hannah knew Mom would be home soon. "You have got to go home, *now*! My mom will be mad that I let a *gremlin* into our house."

"You're my friend!" cried Garry. "I haven't a home to 'go home' to. Can't I stay here with you? We could play every day!"

Hannah heard Mom's car in the driveway. "You can stay until you find a new place, but in the attic where Mom won't see you."

"Don't worry, my friend," Garry said. "She won't know I'm here. I'll be invisible."

But Garry didn't stay in the attic.

And, he didn't come down to play.

In a few days Hannah's mother sat down across the breakfast table, the 'I'm worried' look on her face. "Sweetheart, have you been sleeping well?

"Of course mom." It was a lie. She had heard Garry in the attic.

Her mom went on. "I've been hearing odd noises at night. Strange things too. The TV was on this morning when I got up, and my lunch was missing from the fridge."

"Well honey, let's not worry about it." And with that she kissed Hannah on the forehead and went to work.

Hannah started to get angry. I mean...really angry.

Being blamed for all of Garry's tricks was too much! So she went up into the attic and what do you think she saw?

A baby gremlin! Not only that, as she went up the stairs she saw more stuff that didn't belong. There were her crayons (spilled out all over the attic floor), with baby bites in them. Her coloring books were full of green scribbles, and there was her kickball, as flat as can be. There were other things she had never seen before: a recliner, a big TV with a remote control, video games, and loads of gremlin garbage. And what else? The leftovers...or what was left of them. It was a mess and smelled yucky!

Garry appeared. Then he walked to the recliner and to the video games. Hannah yelled, "What about finding a new place? Now my house is a stinky mess!"

"Oh, Hannah, don't worry. I'll clean it. Let me finish my game."

"But, Garry, I thought friends shared time together. Let's go to the park to play," she begged. "It's no fun alone."

"I *am* your friend," said Garry, "for real! Now go outside and play. Get some fresh air. I'm busy. And could you bring me up some cereal?"

Hannah went to the park. Her heart felt heavy and she started to cry. She got there, sat on a bench, and just hung her head. After a while she heard a voice say, "I suppose you're wondering why I'm so green."

An old lady gremlin, knitting nearby, smiled at her.

"You've got gremlins in your life," the old lady noticed. Hannah nodded. The old lady asked, "Did you invite them to stay there?"

Hannah nodded again.

"And....?"

"Well, he's not acting very friendly," Hannah said. "He was supposed to stay invisible, play with me every day, and be my friend."

"Gremlins say anything to get what they want. They turn up from nowhere, ask to be your friend, and do nothing more than leave you with a broken heart and a mess to clean up," said the old gremlin.

She continued, "Do you see those children playing over there?" Hannah smiled. "They play and get along. Are you so very different from them?"

"I'm the *new kid*. They won't like me," said Hannah.

"Listen, you *are* the *new kid*! You have stories they've never heard and been places they've never seen! You're special. New is exciting, but it takes a little getting used to."

Hannah grinned. A little girl across the park smiled back. "See that?"

Hannah asked. "She smiled at me."

"I'll bet she thinks you'd make a good friend," said the old lady.

"I am a good friend," said Hannah, "and I am special!"

"Don't forget the gremlin in your attic. You invited him in, so *you* must invite him out," she said as she faded away.

Once home, Hannah called out, "I'm coming up, Garry," Hannah said as she climbed the stairs. The attic smelled worse than before. Piles of gremlin garbage were everywhere. The baby had become...a little *monster*."

"I'll take care of it," said Garry from behind the recliner.

"Too late, Garry," she said. "I invited you in, now I invite you *out*!"

"Don't do this," he cried. "Look! We can play here. You like to play." The gremlin shouted, "Please, Hannah, don't do this or...I won't be your friend!"

"I know now you are *not* my friend, Garry," Hannah said proudly. "I have real friends who will not lie to me and will keep their promises. My *real* friends smile at me because I'm special, not just to get their way. You go, now, or I'll tell my mom."

Garry's arms dropped to his side, his fists clenched, a snarl curled on his face. He opened his mouth as if to scream and began to spin in place. The very air around him glowed in shades of green, with bits of fur flying everywhere. And then he was gone, and not just Garry, with him went the baby gremlin monster, the recliner, the video games, the remote control, the TV.

All that was left up there was the stinky old gremlin garbage. Hannah was happy to take it out. It reminded her that some things are special and others you need to throw out, before they stink up your attic or break your heart.

After that, she went to play with her new friends—her *real* friends—and never invited another gremlin to stay in the attic again.

The Clever Builder's Daughter

Sarah Pauling

Once upon a time—or, as the kingdom people say: "There were gods in the sea, and they watched us."

There were gods in the sea and they watched us, the story starts, and we find ourselves in the midst of a heat wave in a very old island kingdom; before people learned to fly, before the mountain giants came down and granted wisdom to the common folk, and before the moon shone bright over the Vast Cliffs.

There was a beautiful young woman—a princess, I think it was—and she fell in love with a clever builder's daughter. Not right away, of course. In fact, they weren't too fond of each other at first. They met by chance at a warrior's tournament held in the princess's honor.

Both were too young to fight, but they both *loved* betting games and would place bets on their favorite warriors. Only problem was, they kept on placing bets on opposing fighters. They would argue with one another:

"My warrior is better!"

"No, mine! You might be my princess, but you're not so smart!"

During the very last fight of the tournament, everything changed. They accidentally bet on the same warrior, and that warrior won the day! The happy princess and the happy builder's daughter went to the celebration feast and ended up dancing all night together.

The princess watched the builder's daughter's curly black hair whirl around all pretty while they danced. She listened to the builder's daughter talk about training to one day build houses and castles and shoemaker's shops. The princess decided then and there that she would be happy to marry this clever girl who knew how to create wonderful things with her hands.

Thoughtful Young

The kingdom people didn't give each other engagement rings. Instead, the princess showed her love by giving the builder's daughter a beautiful jewelry box made from the wood of a Tifter tree (which I don't need to tell you is a pretty big deal). With that, they were engaged to be married.

However, things never stay peaceful for long in these old stories. Not long before the marriage was set to occur, a terrible monsoon came roaring into the island country. This monsoon had a name, too, so you *know* it was trouble. The kingdom people called it Crook-Eye in their language, and it came back every fourteen years to demand payment from the royal family.

Now, normally monsoons are just terrible tropical storms, and they don't know how to think and talk for themselves. But ol' Crook-Eye was smart, and a real nasty thing, too. He would rip into the houses on the coastline, destroying everything in sight, unless the queen or king came down to reason with him and offered up part of the kingdom's treasure.

Because of the heatwave, this year was a poor year for farmers, fishermen, and traders all. Everybody in the island kingdom was struggling just to get by. So there just wasn't enough gold or pearls or jewelry to make Crook-Eye happy! Enraged, he captured the princess as punishment. He swept her up in a great gust of wind and carried her away to his palace at the bottom of the ocean. He told her she would have to live there for the rest of her days.

This did *not* make the clever builder's daughter happy. Not being the type to take things lying down, she resolved to save the princess any way she knew how. She went to the queen and king to get their blessing on her mission. They were hesitant at first: they had come to know the builder's daughter and loved her dearly. They didn't want to lose her, too.

"But I can do it," the builder's daughter said. "I'll make a bet with you. I'll bet a thousand and four years of my life I can bring the princess—your daughter—home again."

"That's a big bet," they told her. "Choose your words carefully."

"I mean it," the builder's daughter said. "I'll bring her home, even if I have to live for one thousand years to do it."

The king and queen relented. They gave her fourteen stars they had collected from the night sky. They told her she couldn't look at them yet: she had to keep them locked tight in her jewelry box until she was at her fiancé's prison-palace.

Let me tell you: this girl was something else, if she made it that far without looking inside. I would have looked right away.

The builder's daughter mixed up some beeswax and special tree sap, popped it in her mouth, and blew a gigantic bubble she could stick her head inside to breathe. Then she grabbed her builder's toolkit, put a bridle on her favorite seahorse, and rode out into the ocean. They dove down into the salty waves, pushing deeper and deeper towards Crook-Eye's palace where it sat in the darkness in the middle of the bottom of the sea.

After many hours of travel, the builder's daughter saw a mermaid trapped in a fisherman's net, thrashing in the deep water with no fishermen in sight.

"Oh, you poor thing!" the builder's daughter said. Carefully she used the axe from her builder's toolkit to free the mermaid from the ropes. "You must have just barely got away."

The mermaid smiled at her with pointed teeth. Her gray hair had seaweed tangled up inside it, and she had a growth on her forehand that looked like a small lantern, or like a deep-sea fish's lure.

"Thank you, leg-girl-thing," the mermaid said in a watery voice. "I am hungry, but you are kind, so I will not try to eat you. Unless you would let me nibble on your nose as a snack?"

This didn't sound reasonable to the builder's daughter, who told the mermaid "no." The mermaid understood—they can be pretty reasonable when politely reminded that nobody likes being eaten.

"You saved me, leg-girl-thing," the mermaid said. She reached down to her sparkling tail and pulled off a scale. "If you hold this scale above your head and flash its light into the darkness, I will always come for you. I will bring my friends. And I will *even* tell them not to eat you, but I can't promise they won't try."

The builder's daughter was touched. "I'll take that bet," she said.

She wanted to thank the mermaid, but without another word her new friend swam fast into the gloom.

Alone, the builder's daughter and her seahorse continued deeper into the water. Soon light from the surface stopped piercing the deep, leaving her in pitch blackness. If she weren't underwater, she could use the fire-torch in her builder's kit, but no dice there. She travelled in darkness for what felt like hours, unsure where she was going, or even which direction was "up." The silence was terrible, pressing in on her delicate ears.

Just when she was beginning to lose hope, balls of light bobbed in the distance. Laughter and music floated towards her. The builder's daughter went to investigate.

She saw giant jellyfish, glowing all pretty in the water. She saw equally giant stingrays circling them, like the stingrays were throwing a bonfire party and the jellyfish were the flames.

"Come dance with us, strange one!" the stingrays told her. They circled her seahorse, pulling her closer. "Come share a story, sing a song!"

"I want to," the builder's daughter said. "But I'm on a mission. I have to keep moving."

"If the story you tell is good enough," the stingrays said, "We will give you a jellyfish to light your way like a lantern."

"I'll take that bet," the builder's daughter said. She opened her mouth and told them an ancient story about love and loss and princes and dragons and ocean waves. She began, as her people always do, with the words: "There were gods in the sea, and they watched us." She ended the story, as most people do, with "The End."

The stingrays loved the story. They laughed and the cried saltwater tears into the ocean, and they begged her not to leave. They loved her even more when she used pliers from her builder's kit to remove a mollusk shell from between the biggest stingray's jaw teeth—it had caused him a mighty pain, and the stingrays had never quite gotten the hang of flossing.

"When will we see you again?" they asked.

"I don't know," the builder's daughter said, "but I have more stories for next time."

They kept their promise: a glowing jellyfish the size of her head floated above her when she left.

After several more hours, the water grew very cold. The builder's daughter shivered and pressed forward.

Something curious rose up beneath her: a giant wall blocked her path. It was made from orange coral, that bumpy sea-surface that usually grows in shallow reefs. Somehow, someone had formed it into a barrier with only a single door to let her through.

She and her seahorse and her jellyfish swam down into the door. Quickly, she realized that the coral walls were twisted up into a maze meant to stop intruders from getting to Crook-Eye' palace.

"We must be nearly there!" she said in excitement.

"Shhh," said a voice. "Quiet, or he'll hear you!"

"Who will?" she asked, looking around.

A large lobster wearing armor sat on a coral wall. "Crook-Eye will! He's up causing trouble on the ocean's surface right now, but he'll be back soon, and he hates being disturbed. If you keep making this racket, he'll get so mad at me I might lose my job!"

"Oh. Are you his guard?"

"Well yes, but I'm only supposed to keep people from disturbing him and making a fuss! If you turn around right now, we won't have any trouble. I'd be happy to let you go if you promise to leave."

"Hmm," the builder's daughter said. She began to sing and talk and recite poetry at the top of her lungs.

Now, you may think it was sort of mean to try to get the lobster-guard in trouble, and I'm inclined to agree. But the builder's daughter knew she couldn't solve the maze alone, and she had a plan.

"Stop it, stop it!" said the lobster. "I'll do anything you ask!"

"Then show me through the maze," the girl said. "If you do that, I promise I won't make any noise at all until I'm out of the maze you're guarding. That way you won't get in any trouble."

The lobster shifted anxiously from one set of feet to another. Finally, he agreed. "Fine!" he said. "But no sounds. Nothing. If you say a single word in the maze, I'm taking you back."

"I'll take that bet," the builder's daughter said.

The lobster was true to his word. He led her carefully through the maze. Just as she promised, the builder's daughter didn't say a word, even when cruel traps would spring just feet in front of them, or when black eels with frightening blind faces would suddenly come streaming out of holes in the wall.

Finally, they made it to the end of the maze. The builder's daughter whispered to the lobster: "Maybe you should get a job where your boss isn't so mean."

"Hmph," the lobster said, crawling back inside his maze.

And there, sitting on the floor of the ocean, was the dark, cold, prison-palace.

The builder's daughter hurried to the walls, where she found a barred window.

"Princess!" she said.

From inside the window, the princess cried out in excitement and fear. "My love!" she said, clutching the bars. "You can't stay here—Crook-Eye will be back any minute!"

"I'm going to get you out of there!"

But before the builder's daughter could even get out her tools to loosen the bars, Crook-Eye came roaring back.

The great, evil typhoon had been flying from island to island, telling people to give up their treasure to him. Now, in the water, he looked more like a whirlpool, with gold and gems spinning around in his center.

"How dare you?" he howled. "The princess is mine! I took her, fair and square!"

"I don't know about that," the clever builder's daughter said. "Care to make a bet with me, Crook-Eye?"

The builder's daughter loved betting games; it was true. But nobody loved betting games more than Crook-Eye.

"I'm listening," he said with a grumble.

She said, "Crook-Eye, I bet you that I can circle around this palace for one thousand and four years straight, without stopping once."

And Crook-Eye said, "No you can't," and she said, "Yes I can," and he said, "Fine, if you can do that then you can take the princess back to the island with you."

"Deal," said the builder's daughter.

"Well? What are you waiting for?"

And the girl said, "Ah-ah-ahhhh, we didn't say when I had to *start.*"

Quick as a flash, she held up her jewelry box at the barred window, right between the princess and herself. She opened it up, and the king and queen's fourteen stars came pouring out. They ran through her hair, danced down her skin, and flashed in her eyes. The same thing was happening to the princess. The stars sang in the two girls' blood and came to rest in their hearts.

Just like that, the builder's daughter knew that she and the princess would easily live for a thousand years.

"Great," Crook-Eye said. "Now you should get started. Start going around the palace."

"Not yet," she said.

The next thing she did was hold up the mermaid's scale. It flashed in the darkness, sending great beams of light up into the water.

For a moment, everything was quiet. Then she heard the lobster-guard's voice saying: "This way! He's a bad boss anyway!"

A flood of merpeople came out of the maze, one after the other, an entire mer-town's worth. They carried with them jellyfish, and they rode on the storytelling stingrays from beyond the maze.

Being a builder's daughter, the girl began to build.

Her friends helped her. They broke down the coral maze wall for parts, and they used it alongside driftwood, pearls, and rocks from the ocean floor. Crook-Eye was furious, of course, but he couldn't do much without interfering with their bet. He'd never do that; it would hurt his pride too much.

It took a long time to build what they needed: years, in fact. The builder girl—because that's what she was, now, a builder in her own right—well, she never lacked people to talk to. And when everyone was resting, the princess would stretch her arms out of the barred window to hold the builder girl's hands. They would laugh and tell jokes and play games. They would talk about the wedding they'd have when they were back on the surface.

And, after two years, the builder girl and her mermaid and stingray friends built a beautiful palace of their own, smaller than the prison-palace, but lighter. The difference was that *their* palace was built with good intentions, so it could float in the water instead of sitting dead-weight on the bottom like the prison-palace did. The builder girl tied the two palaces together, using her fiancé's captivity as an anchor to keep her from floating away.

"Crook-Eye! I'm ready to start circling," she said, standing in her new palace's entrance hall.

Then her mermaid friends gave her palace a big push, which set it moving in the water in a wide arc around the prison-palace. "I'm circling the palace!" she cried out to Crook-Eye. "So there!"

Crook-Eye was spitting mad. He howled, and raged, and screamed, "No fair, no fair!" But he couldn't attack the girl without ruining the bet.

He got so mad that he had to take a long vacation to the northern seas to calm down. He even left his gold and jewels behind in his rush. The merpeople were only too happy to use them to decorate the new palace.

The builder girl hired the lobster-guard, who really needed a new job anyway, to make trips to the island to gather new books and games and maps and tools. He seemed much happier that way.

And so, to this day, the prison-palace sits like a rock at the bottom of the ocean. And, running in small, bold circles around that palace, you can see the little Builder Palace, cobbled together out of stardust and coral and good intentions. It circles the prison-palace as the builder's daughter lives inside, dining and reading and building and betting with her loyal friends. The mermaids like her parties so much, they don't even try to eat her.

She waits for the day she wins her wager with Crook-Eye and can return to the surface.

As her palace passes the princess's window, they can look through and gaze at each other's faces. They talk. Sing. Apologize. Tell stories. Pass notes through the bars. Reach out and take each other's hands. One day they'll be reunited again, and then they'll come back to the island kingdom to take their rightful place as queens.

And that's how the story ends: the two of them circling each other. Trapped, but not unhappy, and never alone. Waiting to go free.

At least, that's how this story used to end. But that thousand and four years went by in a flash for them. The world changed and grew and advanced. If my math is right, their time at the bottom of the ocean is ending...let's see...

Tomorrow.

Thoughtful Young

St. Estevan of the Children

E.E. King

The children, the Angelitos, passed first, treading paths made of marigolds.

The morning after, if you looked closely you could see small footprints in the golden petals. That was why parents always made impressions of their newborn's feet even before they were baptized, pressing sole, heel, and each tiny toe, tenderly into dark ink, then rolling them over white paper, learning by heart the snail-like curves and intricate mazes that marked every individual. That way, if their babies died, they would recognize the tracks their children left when they came home the eve of October thirty-first to spend the day with their families.

When the children returned to their graves on the twilight of November first, the path to the cemetery was marked by golden swirls of petals that had momentarily stuck into the grooves of each tiny foot.

It was Estevan's first time out. He'd been dead just under a year. Perhaps this was why he'd become confused on the way back to the grave.

It was unusual for him to be lost. During his ten years on earth, he'd always been adept at finding missing objects, pets, and people. It was Estevan who spotted lost jewelry sparkling like fallen stars in the dusty fields and discovered the panicky poodles and frightened babies everyone was searching for.

When his abuela, Maria Araceli Dolores' wedding ring slipped from her finger, it was Estevan who spied it glistening in the limestone arroyo like a speck of mica. And when Señor Diaz's youngest daughter, Magdalena Maria Josephina waded into the river and got swept away, it was Estevan who found her clinging to a willow branch more than five hundred meters downstream.

Maria Leticia Laurelita, Estevan's mother, said it was because Estevan had been born on Saint Jude's, patron saint of lost causes, feast day.

Few Christians dare to invoke the name of Jude, for fear that their entreaties might reach Christ's betrayer, Judas, by mistake. Thus, the ignored Jude is eager to assist anyone, and he will intercede even in the direst of circumstances.

Estevan died trying to save a puppy. He'd been drawn to a dry well by cries as plaintive as a baby's no one else seemed to hear. In the bottom of a pit, more than four meters deep, crouched a tiny white dog with curly hair and eyes as big, brown, and soulful as Estevan's own. A stone around the well came loose. Estevan toppled in, smashing his head on the hard stone bottom.

The puppy, though splattered with blood, was unhurt. To everyone's amazement, Maria kept the dog, naming it Vite (little Estevan) in memory of her son.

Now, almost a year after his death, Estevan awoke, leapt from his grave, and hurried after the children weaving through the confusion of old stones and around the hard, bare mounds of dirt hidden beneath elaborate floral displays.

Gliding through the old, black metal gates, Estevan drifted home; drawn by the cries of Vite and the scent of sorrow wafting from his mother's bedroom window.

Inside the kitchen, Maria was placing a dozen tiny loaves of pan de muertos on Estevan's altar. The bread, made with half a dozen fresh eggs, blood oranges, and wild anise seeds, had been salted by tears and sweetened with longing. Tiny sugar-bright icing faces peeped out from between the folds of dough like hidden sorrows.

Even though Vite had only seen Estevan once, the dog leaped up and down, joyfully panting as soon as the boy's spirit drifted through the heavy oak doors.

Estevan glided to the altar, sucking the essence of the bread into his hollow body, nurturing his spirit with his mother's love. He had not eaten for a year, and the bread, even though it was just the spirit of bread, filled him with happiness and made his drowsy. Lying down on his bed, which was made up with freshly laundered sheets that smelled of lavender and devotion, he drifted off into a dream filled sleep, totally unlike the slumber of death.

Generally speaking, the dead do not dream. Instead they lie in a torpor so complete and peaceful, even their flesh melts into repose. But that night, Estevan dreamed of sugar skulls and flying, of mother's kisses and morning light, of playing fetch with small white dogs. Perhaps his dreams, like his discovery skills, were inspired by Saint Jude, for are not dreams the ultimate lost cause? Difficult to remember, impossible to forget, stealing from waking hours, telling stories in the night.

Estevan listened to his dreams. He floated away on reveries, dozing all through the night, into the day and the next day and night beyond. Vite snuggled next to him, warming the memory of his bones.

The days were overcast, and he was so comfortable that although he was supposed to return to the cemetery on November first, he didn't awaken until the third when a stray sunbeam wandered through a rain cloud and shone into his eyes. Then he leaped up hastily, throwing the coverlet onto the floor and startling his mother so severely that if she'd had a weak heart she might have followed him into the grave.

Estevan raced from the house, seeking the path of marigolds, but they were gone, blown away by playful gusts of wind, trampled by burros, and smashed into nothing by cartwheels, tires, and the pounding of many feet.

Estevan turned in circles, whirling like a leaf in a twister, dazed by the light and day. Sun glinted down tinting the afternoon streets with gold, gilding the edges of each cobblestone and pouring through Estevan till he was paler than a mist.

Vite ran after him, but even the most faithful dog cannot see ghosts in daylight. Phantoms navigate by starlight, following the pull of darkness that rises in the dust of their bones like a tide. That is the reason they prefer the night. That is the reason they shun the light.

Maybe he should go back home? Possibly he could crawl under the bed and hide until next year, but it was too late. For the first time in his life or death, he was lost.

Every day that he drifted beneath sunny skies, he dimmed. Each night he remained out of his grave he faded, until by winter solstice, he was less than a twilight haze over still water. And as his ghost dwindled away, all recollections of him diminished, for no matter how strong love is it cannot remember a daylight ghost.

It was probably Estevan's last night on earth. In the morning, he would be nothing. Then, even his mother would forget the boy she had loved so much, for it is only memory that keeps the dead alive. As he began to disappear, dwindling into darkness, a voice rose out of the night, quavering as uncertainly as light through a storm.

Estevan drifted toward the sound, pulled to something for the first time since he had overslept. On the ground knelt a small, white boy. He was obviously dead. Even Estevan's nonexistent eyes could see that.

"Why are you crying?" he whispered, his voice a tickle in the wind.

The boy looked up, tears forming transparent pathways down his skin.

"I'm lost," he said. "I can't get home. I went to the door, but I couldn't open it and my mother wouldn't let me in." He sobbed, each teardrop washing away more of him.

Estevan laid a gentle hand on the ghost's shoulder. It was like being touched by a breeze.

"Don't you know you're dead?" he asked.

The boy's eyes opened so wide Estevan could see into his soul.

"It's okay," he said. "You can rest now. Sleep quiet in your grave. It's not bad. It's peaceful in the cemetery. Then, rise on October thirty-first, and you can spend the whole day with your family." As Estevan spoke, he grew stronger and more solid.

"Can you show me the way?" asked the ghost boy.

Suddenly Estevan could see the bright pathway of golden marigolds. Their scent filled him with longing. He took the ghost boy by the hand, lucent fingers interlacing like braids of fog, and led him gently to the boneyard.

Now he was back. Estevan thought he'd lay down to sleep, but outside of the old metal gates he heard a cry, soft as sunset. Just outside of the gates knelt a small translucent girl.

"Why are you crying?" Estevan asked. "Are you lost?"

The child stuck a glass-clear thumb into her mouth. Gazing up at him out of wide, night-black eyes she nodded.

"I tried to go home," she lisped. "But Mommy won't let me in. Sh-sh-she didn't even see me."

"Don't you know you're dead?" asked Estevan.

The little girl shook her head. "What's dead?" she said, tongue twisting around her soggy finger.

Gently, tenderly he took the girl's free hand and led her toward her grave.

"It's okay," he said. "Don't worry. Rest now."

"But I'm cold," she whispered.

"If you lie down in your grave, the love of your mother will cover you like a blanket and each November first you can return home and let her memories fill you like a sea of hot chocolate and warm you for another year." He kissed the child softly as she faded back into the earth.

Thus it was that Estevan did not return to the earth that year, or the next, or the next. Instead, he became a guide leading the newly dead down the path of marigolds to sleep. Seven years later, when Vite died, he joined Estevan in searching out and leading the deceased to peace and slumber.

And from that day to this, mothers tell their babies that if ever they lose their way, in this life, or the next, to look for a ghostly boy with a little white dog. Saint Estevan will lead them to safety.

Thoughtful Young

Orrery Games

Russel Hemmell

I haven't made it to Architect yet.

With 57 completed orbits, I'm little more than a child. But I like watching and learning, so I'm faster than the other nestlings at playing the Game.

Grown-ups are never pleased when we indulge in this pastime. They say we don't know enough, and these are not things you should fool around with. *Not before your 200th orbit, kids.* But we never listen; temptation is too strong.

Tonight Eemi, Sahl, and I are going to do it again. Since we are forbidden to touch anything within 1043 parsecs of our borders, we chose a far-away object.

It's a real complete system—with planets, moons, asteroids, and comets–and we can't wait to play with it. It's remote. Its tiniest satellites are barely visible from here, and there's only a medium-size yellow sun to lead them all, which disappoints Sahl slightly. If Eemi is the elder and the Chief Architect-in-training, and I am the Destroyer of Worlds, Sahl is the Artist: she's the one who gives the new configuration the harmony we're all bound to seek and achieve. What can you do with only one (average) parent star to play with? But it's cute, our system, and harmonious even she admits it.

Good fun ahead.

Spherical holograms dance in front of us, glittering and colourful. My vision cones zoom in on a big blue ball tilted on its orbit–frosty look and delicate rings make it fancy. I spring into action, ready to grab and retreat it to the far end of the planet table.

"Wait for your turn, Mika," Eemi barks at me. "First pick is mine. Stick to what you do best."

She makes her move, and a huge, puffy planet full of stripes and an impressive cohort of moonlets advances steadily to the inner center of the system.

"It's never going to work," I reply, putting the giant back to its original place. "It's too massive. It will affect all the small bodies nearby and dislodge the orbits even of the bigger ones."

"But it shouldn't be there either," Sahl says. "Gas planets this size are never that far away from their parent star. I'm sure one of the Elders moved it."

"You mean, for real?"

"Have you ever seen anything like this?"

We both look at Eemi for confirmation. She shrugs, waves her appendages in a circular motion, and what was before a neat table of celestial objects now resembles an ungodly mess. Some of them now spin furiously fast, and a couple of collisions in the moonlet area create a gleaming stream of stardust-quality particles. My own contribution is to grab a small red planet and put it on the orbit of its prettier, bigger twin, a blue kitten with lots of water and plenty of surface features. I discard its big moon though; it's too ugly to be left around. I send it crashing to the asteroid belt nearby. Sorry, missy.

Sahl, always the perfectionist, gives the finishing touch. A few frozen rocks in remote orbits are now packed between the main sequence star that rules this system and its first crater-ridden child. Typically Sahl's—no space wasted; no planet left behind.

We admire our creation for a few moments, happy with the result and rightfully proud. It deserves to be made real, this one. We all shift into wavelength form, waiting for Eemi's signal. Three, two, one...

"Let's start."

It's my turn now. I start rotating faster and faster, sending gravitons and ripples through the space-time fabric that will change those remote worlds forever.

Now all we have to do is wait, with rightful expectation and moderate anxiety, for the impact waves to cross the neighboring Orion Arm's interstellar void and reach the system. We're going to see gutted rocks flying around, matter devoured by the white holes I called into existence, and a brave new system to be born-

"Enough, kids. Time to stop."

Elder Ad, Eemi's creator, shows up in her filament light incarnation. Not her physical presence, but she doesn't need one to talk to us. Ad stops my energy waves and recalls them back to our nest, amid our miffed cries and squeals of disappointment.

"But we created a magnificent new system. Look at that!" I say, showing her our masterpiece hovering in the Game Hall. "Why can't we go on?"

"It looks good, Mika, I concede. But it can be inhabited," she says. "In this way you will annihilate whatever life exists in there. Have you considered this possibility?"

"Can't be," Eemi says. "We'd know by now. They would have contacted us in some ways, like the others have."

"What if it is a primitive lifeform? One that hasn't managed yet to deal with galactic time-distance," Ad replies. "One that still believes it's alone in the universe."

"Whatever," Sahl says. "If there's life in this system, it's one that can't work with us anyway. It has no value."

"Maybe not." Ad's light becomes more brilliant, her wavelength shifting to the ultraviolet. "But the system is still young, less than five billion years. It might be growing. You'll need to be patient, children. One day, sentient beings from those planets might be able to reach us."

Eemi doesn't seem convinced, but she obeys. The holographic system slowly recedes to its original shape, moonlets coming back to their former orbits and the planet with the most beautiful rings I have ever seen claiming its former place on the table. The rightful king. The red planet abandons forever its blue sibling's neighborhood, while the ugly moon regains its right to existence, reassembling from a cloud of debris. But my favorite, the tilted blue planet, is no longer threatened by the puffy one. When I think about this, I'm not so unhappy we've been stopped.

"So there's nothing we can do about this system?" Sahl asks.

"Yes," Ad says. "You can attempt communication."

Eemi and Sahl look dubious and eventually decide against it. What's the interest in primordial life, anyway? They leave, and I remain alone in the Orrery Game Hall, observing the system we played with. My friends are wrong: it's not useless, it's beautiful. That is all it needs.

Mika might well be the Destroyer, but she can be a Kind One, too.

I'll give you a gift, pretty baby system. I tell myself that if there's a species over there, however primitive, able to observe the outer space, it might appreciate, and understand where it comes from. Or maybe not; mine is wishful thinking as many others, but one that makes me feel good.

I gently lift one of our system's sun grazing comets, glowing in a white-hot light, and I put it into the direction of the yellow star, ready to get captured as soon as gravity is strong enough.

Lift off.

Its tail leaving a shimmering ice plume, a silver mark on its oddly shaped body, my comet starts its long voyage to the system of moonlets and rings, carrying a silent message of friendship.

Walking the Thrice Blessed Road

Tais Teng

"Always, always stay on the main road," Mago's mother warned him for at least the third time. "The wise Plautos blessed the very stones of this road. No once, not twice, but thrice! And because of that, only true humans can walk it. The moment a monster puts a filthy claw or hoof on that road, they are incinerated by magic fire. Turned into drifting ash." She said that with a certain relish. Mago's mother had little use for monsters and abominations.

"I am not going to do anything stupid," Mago sputtered. Great gods, how his mother could rattle on. "I am twelve, mother. Four more years and I will be allowed to marry or enlist in the army."

"You don't set a single step on the grass. You march right to our neighbor and deliver our pregnant goat."

"Yes, Mother," Mago sighed. "With my eyes looking straight ahead and never missing a step."

"And you certainly shouldn't marry anyone without asking me and your father first." His mother always wanted to have the last word.

The road to High Poseidonis was centuries old, paved with massive plates of snow-white marble. A mile beyond Mago's farm, a dense forest began, filled with furtive rustlings and intriguing creaks. The goat followed Mago with a swaying belly and halted at every third clump to nibble the sea-thistles. Mago tugged at the cord, but it could as well have been fastened to the kind of boulder cyclops liked to throw at passing triremes.

"Most annoying isn't she, such a goat?" a voice said. "I know all about it, because I'm half-goat myself."

The faun squatted on a tumbled pillar. He had horns on his head and indeed the legs of a goat. He raised a collar glittering with emeralds. "Put this collar around her neck, and she'll follow you. As meek as a lamb."

"Yes, and now I am supposed to step from the road to get your nice present?" Mago snorted. "You think I'm simple or something? The moment I leave the road, you jump me."

"Us goats, we eat about anything, true, but never humans. Catch!" The collar sailed through the air and landed at Mago's feet. "Have fun with it!"

Mago stared at the collar. It looked quite expensive, studded with sparkling jewels and gleaming pearls. It and the rope rested on the blessed pavement without turning into ash, so there was nothing wrong with it. Mago picked up the collar and fastened it around the neck of the goat. He tried a tentative tug, and o wonder! The goat followed without a single bleat or backwards tug.

"I wove that collar and the rope from the very best burdock plants. It sticks to anything, and only a magic sword can ever cut that rope."

"What?" Mago cried. He snatched his hand back and shook it, but the rope seemed to have bonded with his very skin. Perhaps even with his bones.

"Hacking off your hand is an option, of course." The bushes rustled and the faun was gone.

The collar shimmered and turned into a wreath of coarse leaves and hooked seeds. The pearls became ordinary dewdrops. Mago tugged at the cord, but the sticking part of the magic held.

Never take a present from a stranger, his mother had always told him. He sighed. This time, this one time, she was proved right.

"And what do I see?" a voice shrilled from high in the sky. "A nice stuffed goat with a boy as my dessert!"

A harpy wheeled above the road. She had the scrawny feather-mop body of a vulture and the face of the worst kind of witch. The kind of witch that catches and cooks toddlers, not the Circe kind that seduces young men and only turns them into swine when they don't satisfy her. Her chin and hooked nose almost touched. Between them gaped a maw filled with shark teeth. A split snake-tongue licked her black lips.

"This road is blessed, no-grandmother-of-mine!" Mago taunted her. "The moment you land, your feathers will burst into flame."

"Now, why should I ever land?" the harpy asked. "I'll just catch you in my claws and fly you to my nest!" She dived like an eagle, and her claws closed on Mago's left arm. Mago's feet left the ground. He screamed like a scalded piglet, kicking his legs and seeking for purchase that simply wasn't there. The rope with the goat became as taut as a bow string, and Mago halted in midair.

"Let go of that stupid rope, you dumb dessert!" the harpy shrilled. "You and the goat, I can't lift such a weight."

"Impossible!" Mago wailed. "The rope is stuck to my hand. Held like a bird on a glue-stick."

"What rubbish!" She put Mago with a bump on the ground, alighted on the still-taut rope, and bit deep into the fibers. A panicky flapping followed.

"Let me go!" It sounded rather muffled. Both her lips and her feet were glued to the rope. Only by frantically beating her wings she kept from touching the deadly road.

Mago clacked his tongue and continued on his way, with the goat and the wailing harpy following him. He dearly hoped his neighbor knew a remedy for a harpy and an enchanted rope.

The bushes rustled once again.

"Sir Faun?" Mago hopefully asked, "is that you again?"

A man jumped on the grassy verge, brandishing his sword. "Your goat or your life!" he roared. "Or no, I'll take them both. I haven't killed anybody this week yet."

Mago folded his arms. He felt astonishing calm. He must have used up all his fear with the harpy.

"This road is blessed. Every monster that steps on the road will instantly be incinerated."

"Some people called me a monster, but I'm just a bad man." He peered in a rather myopic way at the flapping harpy, blinked. "If you think I'm afraid of your tame vulture..." He stepped on the road and nothing happened. His sandals didn't ignite, and neither did the rest of this body.

What the heck, Mago thought. *He really is just a human.*

The robber grabbed the rope with the goat, shook his hand, and frowned. "Now what's this sticky stuff?" He raised his sword.

"Your sword?" Mago hopefully asked. "Is it perhaps..." The sword touched the rope and was instantly glued down. "You don't have to answer. I see it isn't magical at all."

Tugging the pregnant goat, the wailing harpy, and the cursing bandit, Mago walked on. Thanks to the enchanted rope, everybody followed him meek as a lamb. Compared to the recalcitrant goat at the start of the journey, this walk was almost peasant, he decided. As long as he wasn't devoured or cut into pieces the moment the faun's spell failed.

The road made a sharp bend and ended in a brand-new bridge across a swollen river. This was the spring flood, straight from the melting snow, making the river impossible to ford. Mago heard the waters roar, the rattling of rolling boulders. During the summer the road just continued across the dry riverbed.

Mago's steps faltered. Below such suddenly-appearing bridges, some rather unpleasant folks were rumored to live. Creatures who often asked for a rather high toll before allowing a traveler to cross.

I don't have much choice, he decided and stepped on the planking of the bridge.

A voice seemed to bubble up straight from the river: "Whoever crosses the Bridge of Great Charybdis will have to pay my toll. The life of the last person to cross the bridge belongs to me."

"That seems fair," Mago said. He was the one in front and had nothing to fear. The bandit however yelped and then forced his way past the goat.

The moment Mago reached the other side of the river an arm made from gray, swirling water rose from the river and grabbed the goat by her hind-legs.

"Now what is this, in Poseidon's name?" the voice burbled. "My hand seems to be stuck to that goat!"

Trailed by a harpy, a highwayman, a pregnant goat, and a wailing whirlpool, Mago finally arrived at the marble villa of his neighbor.

The neighbor stood in front of his gate and shook his head in wonder. "Well, as sure as my name is Plautos, this is the most marvelous procession I've ever seen!"

"Plautos?' Mago asked. "As in Plautos the Wise who blessed this road? Enchanted it to burn all monsters who might bother an honest traveler?"

"I am indeed that Plautos and some folk call me wise, but I laid that enchantment a rather long time ago. It stopped working some three centuries back."

"Oh," Mago said with a very small voice. "But do you perhaps own a magic sword?" He raised his hand to show the enchanted rope.

"Most certainly. I never close the door behind me without taking a magic sword."

The stretched rope snapped at the first stroke. The harpy flapped screeching up into the sky, but not without first grabbing the bandit in her claws. The whirlpool dived gurgling in Plautos' dry well and left only a trail of droplets gleaming in the moss.

Plautos, whom some folks called "The Wise" folded his arms and looked down on Mago. "And what did you learn from all this?"

"Uh, never trust your mother if she calls something safe?"

Thoughtful Young

Buyer Be-Were

Elizabeth Ann Scarborough

Werewolves were the farthest thing from my mind as I fell asleep halfway across Wyoming. In the front seat, my mom nodded and made noises in the right places while my stepdad-wannabe crowed about how brilliant he had been to get them in on the "ground floor" of this amazing new housing opportunity.

All I knew was it was a long way from Denver, where my *life* was, our home- sweet-cruddy-apartment-home, my school, and the critters I volunteered to help with at Friends in Need Animal Shelter.

I didn't know if Mom was in love with Jasper Hogg or not, but after the years since my dad died, when she worked two, sometimes three, minimum-wage jobs to pay the bills, I guess he looked pretty good. He wasn't exactly movie star material, but he talked a lot about how much money he made as a real estate developer and how much he worked out.

He kept sending Mom bouquets and taking her to fancy places there was no way we could afford to set foot in. I must say the doggy bags were delicious. Mom hadn't had much time to date, but she's gorgeous. I look more like my dad, who wasn't.

The downside about Jaspar's money was he bragged. He bragged a *lot*. Every conversation became about his position as a partner of this real estate development corporation, especially lately, when they'd closed this humongous deal with the government. And now we were going to Wyoming.

"It's paradise!" he told us before we began the drive. "It has everything. Views of beautiful scenery, fantastic night skies, access to hot springs pools, good hunting and fishing, horse riding, and it will have schools and churches soon."

Now he slowed as we passed a billboard advertising, "Park View Heights, an Exclusive Gated Community for

Executive Homeowners. A Swinson, Boarly, and Hogg Development." He made us get out for pictures.

The place looked familiar and when I heard Mom gasp, I knew she had recognized the area too. In spite of the fences, the cleared ground, the fake lawns and the smells of sawdust and insect spray mingling in the air with a soupcon of sulfurous stink, this was where Dad had brought us for our only summer vacation ever. Back then, it was part of a national park.

Jaspar waved his arms around to the trees, the mountains in the distance, the shining lake beyond, and the sprawling plains speckled with elk and buffalo. "We get to enjoy all of this. There's still time to enjoy all the property has to offer. The big predators have been eliminated, leaving the tasty ones for the people who can pay to play. Because of the natural geothermal energy we tap into there are no power bills to worry about even in the winter."

Just then, down in the valley, a spume of water shot into the air. Once a world-famous geyser. "Don't worry about that," Jaspar said. "People will pay to see it after we fix it. Engineers are working on it right now; they say they can re-plumb it so it's not in the way. So. Ready to move in?"

He had to shout over the noise of hammers and saws and heavy machinery. Most of the houses around us were unfinished frames, while many others looked just like the one he herded us into—fake stone to about doorknob height and then wood painted white. Two stories. Yippee.

"It's k-kind of isolated," Mom said.

"That's because we're the first ones here. And you'll be too busy to notice, baby. I got you a job as receptionist in the office. Most of the houses are already sold, so we'll be getting neighbors soon, and I'll be in and out of the office too. And there'll be builders, carpenters, plumbers, electricians, gardeners, and surveyors on-site during the day."

Great. That sounded like lots of company, though not the fun kind.

He made the mistake of turning to me. "So what do you think, Izzy?"

"I think I want to stay with Grandma and keep going to school at home," I told him.

"You kids, always so scared of change," he said. "You'll be happy to know that the wi-fi is excellent and you can telecommute to the high school in Jackson until we have enough kids here to build one."

Grandma? I'm coming home!

"Now, you girls go freshen up. My partners will be arriving soon and we'll have a big barbecue. You ever tried buffalo burgers, Iz?"

"I'm a vegetarian," I told him, which I hadn't been until just then.

It had turned cold by the time we got outdoors. Two houses down, a picnic table was set with a tablecloth and piles of plastic silverware and paper plates. A small clique of people wearing expensive-looking outdoor-wear waved at Jaspar, who pulled Mom over to meet them, and introduced me. "This is Mr. and Mrs. Swineson, our senior partners."

"Carl and Karen," Mr. Swineson said.

"And Mrs. Boarly and her husband Jeffrey." I nodded.

A dark haired boy who looked to be about my age was manning the grill. I walked over. "You got any veggies maybe?" I asked him.

He grinned at me and turned so I could read his tee-shirt which said that vegetarian was an old Indian word for lousy hunter.

"Very funny," I said. "I don't hunt at all actually. So do you?"

"Hunt? Oh yeah."

"No, I mean, do you have any veggies?"

"How about corn and a potato?" he suggested.

"Great, thanks. Do you live around here?"

"I'm the hired help. Or my mom is. So far my salary is under negotiation. But they'll pay me for sure. Not many folks want to come out here to work now."

"Let me guess. Because your bosses plan on turning the park into a tacky neighborhood for rich retirees?"

"Smart girl."

Maybe I should have kept my mouth shut.

"Is Hogg your dad?"

"Nope. He's running for stepdad, or at least, he wants to marry my mom."

"I'm sorry. I'm Ezra, by the way."

"Isabelle—Izzy. I seem to be stuck here. No offence."

"None taken. I'm stuck here too, but it's where I grew up." His mouth quirked and there was a humorous twinkle in his brown eyes. *Maybe this arrangement could be tolerable after all.*

When Mom, Jasper, and I got back to the new house, a waterfall was running down the wall, turning the hallway into a river. We shoved the boxes that were either wet or in danger of getting wet into other rooms while the wall-to-wall bubbled and soaked. Jaspar called the on-site plumbers.

That was just the first disaster. In the next two weeks, it was one after another. Three fires broke out in one night. When the crew got ready to install windows, they found most of them were broken. Other plumbing accidents soaked the dry wall.

One night Jasper came stomping into the house, obviously peeved. "It looks like some feral dogs or something got into the insulation and peed and cra—," he looked at me as if I had never heard the word before, "—pooped all over it. We had to re-order almost the entire shipment."

"Bummer," I said but that night, I left the window to my room cracked, interested in the dogs. Maybe I could make friends with one.

In my sleep, I heard a muffled whimper and told myself to wake up. Sure enough, the whimper was real, and so was the answering whine. A few yips followed. I looked out the window and could see something moving near the deep shadows cast by the framed-in house across the road. Was there a hurt dog out there? From the sound, it could even be a puppy! Poor thing. I ran downstairs in my pajamas and opened the front door. If the animal was injured, maybe I could help it.

But the noise stopped as if I had smothered it when I stepped outdoors. I heard my breath going in and out, my heart thumping. Nothing moved and though I stood shivering for a moment in the chilly night, I heard no more canine noises.

"Jaspar?" I asked him the next morning, totally freaking him out since I mostly ignored him as much as I could. "You said something about feral dogs. Have you seen any? How do you think they got here? I bet people came out here and dumped them and drove off and left them." At the shelter, I met lots of pets whose owners just abandoned when they became inconvenient.

"Don't get any ideas, Izzy. I haven't seen any actual dogs, just the damage. If you see some, don't approach them. When dogs go wild, they can pack up and be dangerous—they've even killed people, especially kids."

"I've seen people set out live traps before for the TNR trap, neuter, return program for feral cats," I said. "I could help catch them."

"I don't have time to mess with this now, Izzy. Some of our most important and influential backers are coming in a couple of days, and the way things have been going, we won't be anywhere near ready. We don't need any other problems, so just do me a favor and stay out of this. I have a 12 gauge that can deal with those wild mutts fine as soon as I get the time. And I'm sure the building crews will be only too happy to get a little target practice in exchange for permission to bag a buffalo or an elk."

"No!" I said, and decided then and there that no way was my mom marrying this jerk, money or no.

But Mom had overheard us as she entered the kitchen looking for *her* morning coffee, and said, "Izzy. I'm sure Jaspar and his partners know best about these things. It's not the same out here as it is in the city."

That night again, I heard noises, stuff falling, breaking, more little yips, the sudden hiss and gurgle of a garden hose. Maybe there was another fire? Maybe someone needed help? I envisioned a fire and a bucket brigade. But when I heard human voices, they were calm and quiet, one of them a little familiar. The weather was drizzly with a little wind that kept me from making out what they were saying, but it seemed like whatever woke me was over, so I went back to a restless sleep.

The next day, the whole place was buzzing, literally, with heavy equipment, SUV's, trucks pulling horse trailers, and the three-wheelers people used to get around the off-road places in the park. I threw on jeans, a tee, and my hoody, and went out to see what the big deal was.

Ezra rolled by on a three-wheeler. "Hey, Ezra," I called, waving to him. "What's up?"

He waved back and stopped in front of me. "The bigwigs are coming tomorrow. The bosses decided to throw a picnic down by the lake and a trail ride for those who want it. Between you and me, they're probably hoping to distract our visitors from the fact that the project is way behind schedule."

"That almost sounds kinda fun, but I wanted to ask you about something."

"Yeah?"

"Jaspar says they think some of the damage is being done by wild dogs. He wants to kill them."

"Don't worry about it," Ezra told me with a grin. "They haven't survived out here with wolves and coyotes by being stupid."

"But they're going to kill them, Ezra. Jaspar said so."

"Um-hmm," he said. "They can try."

The VIPs arrived around mid-afternoon the following day. Jaspar, the Boarlys and the Swinesons met them at the road.

Mr. Swineson, decked in rugged khakis and plaid shirt met them. "We decided to do the sightseeing tour now, while the light's still good enough to see some of this area's special features and how we propose to adapt them for the use of the residents. For those of you who would like a little exercise, the horses have arrived, and our groom will help you find the right mount."

I was all over that. I used to help a friend exercise her horses. I honestly don't know why people ever traded them in for cars.

After a short trail ride to see the big geyser, the gold rimmed deep blue acid pool, and the oil-slick rainbow mud pots, we headed back to the picnic ground. The broad meadows, it seemed to me, were getting a little bare and no wonder. There was a lot of land, but in places the bison were so thick you couldn't see the grass. Ezra said, "The wolves and other predators used to keep the herds thinned out, which gave the grass a chance to grow and kept the soil from sliding down the hills and into the streams, choking the fish. So there's more bison and elk but less for them to feed on."

The camp faced the lake. The work crews rode three-wheelers down to join us for dinner. It was as good as it smelled, with corn on the cob, potatoes baked in coals, fresh berries and salad, and lots of booze for the guests, the better to loosen their purse strings. Jaspar, Boarly, and Swineson sort of spoiled it talking about how they planned to "improve" the place.

A super-moon, big as a Ferris wheel, rose over the hills beyond the lake, casting a shining trail across the water.

Everything was perfect until people started changing into wolves.

The horses were the first to sense it, stamping and snorting even before the first howl. Then they neighed, bucked, breaking, and galloping away, some of the picnickers chasing them.

Until they noticed that there were wolves among us.

"Everybody get to your cars." Someone shouted.

"I thought you guaranteed there were no wolves or bears? I want my money back!" said a lady, breaking into a squeal as one of the wolves nipped her on the calf.

The wolves did not look like German Shepherds, huskies, or any other kind of dog.

They were bigger, for one thing, and mangy looking, You could see their skin through the thin fur spiking along their spines. Their fangs dripped. When wolves were allowed in the park, they must have been well looked after. Some of them had gold fillings.

Someone fired off a shot, and a wolf yelped. People ran toward the parking lot, but even from the campsite we heard the snarls and growling and were almost trampled as the guests stampeded back again and commandeered the three-wheelers.

Wolves ripped through the back of the tent as the first riders roared out of camp.

"The houses! The houses!" Someone else, I think it might have been Mr. Boarly, screamed.

Somehow there were plenty of three-wheelers for all the buyers who'd ridden horses before, but I didn't see a solitary crew member, except Ezra, who skidded his three-wheeler to a stop beside me. "Izzy! Climb on!" I hopped up behind him and we roared down the road.

"Oh nooo," someone cried, "Get away! Eeeeeek! Ow!"

As we passed, I caught just a flash of one of the ladies being dragged off her three-wheeler. The road was too full of other three-wheelers, cars, and wolves for Ezra to turn without hitting someone or dumping our ride on its side. Shrieks, vrooming, and howling filled the night.

There were so many wolves now. Jaspar, struggling with sticking door, pushed into our house. But Mom? I searched the night. There she was, by Swineson's Prius, helping Mrs. Swineson, who was limping. Two wolves grabbed for them and Mom lashed out with Mrs. Swineson's purse smacking them both on their noses as she half-dragged Mrs. Swineson towards the door.

A crash of breaking thermopane glass and Jaspar appeared at the window with his shotgun. He fired and a dimpled pattern appeared on the Prius.

"Stop shooting, you fool!" Mom screamed at him. "Can't you see there's still people out here? Izzy!"

Suddenly everything went dark as, with a screech of tires, somebody hit a streetlamp. All I could see now was wolves, the flashing roar of gunfire fazing them not even a little bit.

I moved to run for the house but Ezra pulled at my arm. "Don't. You're okay where you are. Stay put."

I didn't feel okay. The gunshots finally stopped, but none of the wolves seemed hurt although they began to howl.

I wasn't as surprised as I should have been when Ezra, although still human, threw back his head and howled along with them.

I 'd been noticing more little things about the wolves. A tool belt hanging low from the middle of one, the tattered remains of a Hawaiian shirt I had seen earlier on one of the crew fluttering from furry shoulders. Watches flopped around the paws of two of the bigger wolves. What looked like a pedometer was strapped to the back paw of another one.

"So, some of the wolves were our crew members and the backers?" I asked Ezra. But he had climbed off the bike and was facing the window of "our" house, where everyone had clustered.

"Hey, Mr. Hogg," he called. "Mr. Swineson and Boarly. All you little rich pigs, come out or let us in." Ezra shouted.

"Not by the hair on your chinny-chin-chins," Jaspar said, nodding toward the watching wolves. "What do you want, kid?"

"I want our old pack back, but you had to kill them, didn't you, to make your 'improvements' on our home? I guess you didn't know that some of us were only part-time wolves. Some of us walk on two legs during the day, and those murderers you let loose on our family didn't get us. We can't beat you, so you'll have to join us. You better be glad your bullets don't work on our kind, Hogg, because without knowing it, you could kill some of your biggest backers, though the workers are in no danger."

"They're werewolves? What about you, boy? Why haven't you changed?"

"Because I'm the spokeswolf—what the mob movies call the *consigliare*, capice? So here's the deal, you come out, or we come in. It doesn't matter to us, and we give you each a little nip—nobody has been killed tonight yet, by the way. They're all either inside with you or out here. But if you don't change, we'll huff and we'll puff, and we've got dynamite enough to blow your house down and you all to kingdom come."

After a long silence, the front door creaked open.

"And that was how the apex predators returned to their rightful place in this park and the park was saved from the greedy pigs without anybody involved getting eaten. Ezra finally received his bite of passage, and the full moon smiles on him as on the rest of his pack. And they all lived happily ever after."

"That was a great story, Ranger Izzy," the little girl in the Cardinal Scout uniform said. "But Ranger..."

"Yes?"

"I just want to say how funny it looks to see a wolf in bear's clothing.'"

Thoughtful Young

The ranger grabbed her Smokey Bear hat and clapped it on over her ears and the upper part of her pigtails. "My bad. Now, who wants to howl?"

Contributors

Ahmed Khan's works have appeared in *Boston Review, Strange Horizons, Interzone, Anotherealm*, and more. His stories have been translated into German, Finnish, Greek, Croatian, Polish, and Urdu. Links to published works can be found at http://ahmedakhan.blogspot.ca.

Aimee Ogden is a former science teacher and software tester; now she writes stories about sad astronauts and angry princesses. Her work has also appeared in *Analog, Fireside*, and *Beneath Ceaseless Skies*. With Bennett North, she co-edits *Translunar Travelers Lounge*, a zine of fun and optimistic speculative fiction.

Allan Rousselle graduated from Cornell University with a degree in Russian and Soviet Studies the same year that the Soviet Union disintegrated, and his Master's in Political Science from University of Pennsylvania was immediately ignored when he entered a career in software engineering and data analytics. Allan currently lives in the Seattle area with his three sons. For more of Allan's writing, visit his personal website at http://www.rousselle.com/allan/.

Alphayo Opiyo is a freelance writer majoring mainly on kid's stories and educational pieces. As an upcoming writer he has been able to write various touching and appealing stories such as "She is Living in Fear, When the Sun Rises among many others. Alphayo can be found on story sasa.com or my Facebook page: George Opiyo Sifwototo.

Amy Hammack Turner worked for thirty-eight years as a cataloger for Duke University Libraries, which has a collection of over six million volumes. That experience almost cured her of the desire to add to the vast amount of fiction in the world, but not quite.

Anthea Sharp is the author of the *USA Today* bestselling *Feyland* series. Her short fiction has appeared in numerous anthologies. When she's not writing, she plays Irish fiddle and enjoys the SoCal sunshine with her family.

Avra Margariti is a queer Social Work undergrad from Greece. She enjoys storytelling in all its forms and writes about diverse identities and experiences. You can find her on twitter @avramargariti.

Brian K. Lowe is an active member of the SFWA with over 40 story sales to his credit. His *Stolen Future* trilogy is set in the far future and his *Nemesis* series is set in the 1930s. On Twitter, he is @brianlowewriter, his blog *Graffiti on the Walls of Time* can be found at www.brianklowe.wordpress.com, and his email is brianklowewriter@aol.com. Drop him a note and ask him about his collection of 300 pulp novels.

Donna J. W. Munro has spent the last twenty-one years teaching high school social studies. Her students inspire her every day. She has an MA in writing popular fiction from Seton Hill University. Her first novel, *Revelations: The Poppet Cycle,* will be out in May 2020. Contact her at https://www.donnajwmunro.com or @DonnaJWMunro on Twitter.

E.E. King is a painter, performer, writer, and biologist - She'll do anything that won't pay the bills, especially if it involves animals.

King has won numerous various awards and fellowships for art, writing, and environmental research.

She's been published widely, recently in *Clarkesworld, Flame Tree, Cosmic Roots, and Eldritch Shores* and *On Spec.* One of her tales is on Tangent's recommended reading 2019.

Ray Bradbury called her stories, "marvelously inventive, wildly funny and deeply thought-provoking. I cannot recommend them highly enough."

Her books include *Dirk Quigby's Guide to the Afterlife, Pandora's Card Game, The Truth of Fiction, Electric Detective, The Hollywood Portal, Blood Prism,* and *The Adventures of Emily Finfeather.*

Her landmark mural, A Meeting of the Minds (121' x 33') can be seen on Mercado La Paloma in Los Angeles.

She's worked with children in Bosnia, crocodiles in Mexico, frogs in Puerto Rico, egrets in Bali, mushrooms in Montana, archaeologists in Spain, butterflies in South Central Los Angeles, lectured on island evolution and marine biology on cruise ships in the South Pacific and the Caribbean, and painted murals in Los Angeles and Spain.

Check out paintings, writing, musings, and books at
www.elizabetheveking.com
https://twitter.com/ElizabethEvKing
facebook.com/pages/EE-King
https://www.instagram.com/elizabetheveking
https://whatsinanafterlife.wordpress.com/

Elizabeth Ann Scarborough is the Nebula Award winning author of over forty novels, numerous short stories and editor of three anthologies. In the trilogy she wrote with Anne McCaffrey, a sentient planet shows would-be exploiters that "it's not nice to fool with Mother Nature." This story has a similar theme.

Elizabeth Tuckwell lives in London and currently shares her house with a husband and a lot of books. She enjoys reading and writing all types of science fiction and fantasy. She's a member of the Clockhouse London Writers group. Liz can be contacted by email liz@liztuckwell.co.uk, Twitter @LizTuckwell1, or her website www.liztuckwell.co.uk

Thoughtful Young

I'm **Emily Martha Sorensen,** and I write clean fantasy books that'll make you grin. I've been known to write about mischievous fairies, heroines who can't shut their mouths, and baby dragons in the 1920s. All of my books are clean enough for kids and smart enough for adults. You can find out more about me at http://www.emilymarthasorensen.com!

Han Adcock is a writer of short stories, short long stories, and poetry, residing in Lincolnshire, UK. His work has appeared in such places as *Ink Stains Volume 13* (Dark Alley Press), Rejected (edited by Erin Crocker), and *Creatures* (from Tell-Tale Press). He has a novelette available on Amazon (Damian's Dream) and is the Editor-Illustrator of Once Upon A Crocodile e-zine. Find him at www.facebook.com/wyrdstories or on Twitter (@Erringrey).

Dr. J.C.G. Goetz is a scientist, mathematician, educator, actor, director, playwright, author, and animal lover. He hungers to connect with other people emotionally or intellectually through his work. He may be contacted at indimargm@gmail.com.

James Blakey lives in suburban Philadelphia. His story "The Bicycle Thief" won a 2019 Derringer Award. His website is JamesBlakeyWrites.com.

James Dorr's *The Tears of Isis* was a 2013 Bram Stoker Award® nominee for Fiction Collection. His latest is a novel-in-stories from Elder Signs Press, *Tombs: A Chronicle of Latter-Day Times of Earth.* An Active Member of SFWA and HWA, Dorr invites readers to visit his blog at http://jamesdorrwriter.wordpress.com.

Janka Hobbs grew up in Albuquerque, chasing lizards and feeding bugs to spiders. She now resides among the Puget Sound lowlands, watching slugs feast on mushrooms. The trees here are bigger and less prickly.

Jenny Blackford writes poems and stories for people of all ages, usually with a tinge of myth and legend, science, or deep time. Over 30 of her short stories and over 50 of her poems have appeared in Australian and international anthologies and journals. www.jennyblackford.com

Jessica Artemisia Mathieu writes mystical bedtime stories for all ages, available at JessicaArtemisia.com. She's an inner and outer traveler seeking every kind of treasure to share with anyone who will accept what she has to offer. She lives in Morocco with her canaries and orange tree.

Jillian Sullivan lives in Central Otago, New Zealand. Her twelve published books include novels, essays, short stories, and poetry. A grandmother of nine, she is a passionate practitioner of natural building.

Julie Reeser's current favorite word that sounds like a magic spell is "pestilential." She has work coming soon in *The Future Fire* and *Dreams & Nightmares*, but you can read more of her stuff right now at her Patreon: patreon.com/abetterjulie.

Karen Thrower is an Oklahoma wife and mother. Her story "The Lost Ones" appears in the bestselling anthology *Secret Stairs: A Tribute to Urban Legend.* You can find more of her work on Amazon. amazon.com/author/karenthrower

Karin L. Frank's poems and stories have been published in numerous literary journals and in popular magazines both in the U.S. and abroad.

Ken Grant is a freelance writer living in Santa Ana, California. He has one published novel, *So Great a Salvation.* His short stories have appeared in Alien Dimensions, Jitter Press, and Left Hand Publishers.

Lindsey Morrison Grant is an award-winning author, poet, screenwriter, journalist, photographer, ceramicist, and mixed-media artist from Portland, Oregon. She has been diagnosed with and is actively recovering from Bipolar

Disorder, PTSD, ADD, as well as cancer and heart attack. Twenty years after her initial diagnosis at age 40, she attributes her resilience to her invaluable support network and practicing creative expression in words, sounds, and images.

Michelle F. Goddard is a vocalist/musician who has performed around the world and a composer with credits to her name for songs in musicals and films. She is presently working on several short stories and a science fiction novel. You can find her at michellefgoddard.wordpress.com.

Parker Yancey is a student at Brigham Young University, Idaho, where he is studying Secondary English Education and serves as the current manager of the Writer's Workshop on campus. He writes science fiction and fantasy, and he is currently working on a full-length novel. He loves soundtrack music, animation, and waffles.

Paula Hammond is a best-selling author. She has written over 60 fiction and non-fiction books, as well as short stories, comics, poetry, and scripts for educational DVDs. When not glued to the keyboard, she can usually be found prowling round second-hand books shops or hunkered down in a hide, soaking up the joys of the natural world.

Rebecca van den Ham writes for children and teens. She taught 5th grade before homeschooling her three children. She loves fairy tales and dressing up for any and all occasions. She has been creating stories as long as she can remember and lives with her family and a 20-year-old frog in Southern California. Find her on Facebook @RebeccavandenHamAuthor (https://fb.me/RebeccavandenHamAuthor)

Rob Bachman is a professional guitarist and music teacher. He enjoys reading, Vegan cooking and deciding what to watch on TV. Occasionally his three dogs let him work on stories. He lives in Southern California. This is his first published work.

Rucha Dixit was born and raised in India. After 13 years in the software industry and having both her babies, she realized that she was meant to write. So, she dived straight in and channeled her passion and experience as a new mother into a self-published book, *For New Mums*, on Amazon. Recently, she received an honorary mention from the judges of the SCBWI BAME Scholarship Award for her (unpublished) middle-grade novel. She lives with her husband and two children in London, U.K.

Russell Hemmell is a French-Italian transplant in Scotland after several years of East Asia, passionate about astrophysics, history, and Japanese anime. Winner of the Canopus Awards for Excellence in Interstellar Writing. Recent stories in *Aurealis,* Flame Tree Press, The Grievous Angel, and others. SFWA, HWA, and Codexian. Find them online at their blog earthianhivemind.net and on Twitter @SPBianchini.

Dr. Sara L. Uckelman is an assistant professor of logic at Durham University whose fiction has been published in a variety of journals and anthologies, including Flame Tree Publishing's anthology *Robots and Artificial Intelligence.* Her story in this volume was composed orally on walks to and from school for her daughter, who is super excited that other children will get to read the story, too.

Sarah Pauling sends other people to distant places for a living as a study abroad advisor in Ann Arbor, Michigan. Her work is published or upcoming in *Strange Horizons*, *Cast of Wonders,* and *Abyss & Apex*. If approached without sudden movement, she can be found at @paulings on Twitter, where she natters on about writing, tabletop gaming, comics, and books.

Shelby Workman lives in New Mexico with the world's cutest dog.

Sheila Kerwin is retired faculty of Early Childhood Education. Her poems have appeared in *Hello, High Five,*

Babybug, Ladybug, and *Caterpillar Magazine.* Her blog, Sensiforous, focuses on young children and child development topics. When not working on poetry or picture books, she consults in Early Childhood Education, conducts workshops for teachers, writes piggyback songs, and substitute teaches in local public schools.

Tais Teng: I am a Dutch sf writer and illustrator with the quite unpronounceable name of Thijs van Ebbenhorst Tengbergen, which I shortened to Tais Teng to leave room for a picture of an exploding starship or a clever steam-punk lady on the covers of my novels. In my own language I have written about everything from radio-plays to hefty fantasy trilogies. To date I sold forty-one stories in the English language and two children's books.

Thanks to all of you.
It's been a hoot.
Bob B

Made in the USA
Middletown, DE
10 October 2020

21590075R00139